Four Ex-wives and a Wedding

Steve Higgs

Text Copyright © 2023 Steven J Higgs

Publisher: Steve Higgs

The right of Steve Higgs to be identified as author of the Work has been asserted by him in accordance with the Copyright, Designs and Patents Act 1988

All rights reserved.

The book is copyright material and must not be copied, reproduced, transferred, distributed, leased, licensed or publicly performed or used in any way except as specifically permitted in writing by the publishers, as allowed under the terms and conditions under which it was purchased or as strictly permitted by applicable copyright law. Any unauthorised distribution or use of this text may be a direct infringement of the author's and publisher's rights and those responsible may be liable in law accordingly.

'Four Ex-wives and a Wedding' is a work of fiction. Names, characters, businesses, organisations, places, events and incidents either are the product of the author's imagination or are used fictitiously. Any resemblance to actual persons, living or dead, events or locations is entirely coincidental.

Contents

1. Prologue – The Cake 1
2. Quayside Queue 9
3. The Ex-wives 18
4. Surprise Guest 27
5. Murder 32
6. Shoplifters 39
7. Interview 47
8. Scruffbag 54
9. Risotto 57
10. Saboteur 61
11. Bloodwork 66
12. Lies 70
13. Gate Crasher 76
14. A Small Breakthrough 81
15. A Change in Atmosphere 84
16. Too Tired 89

17.	Glasses and Silverware	94
18.	Lady Mary Turns Sleuth	103
19.	Body Count	107
20.	Unavoidable Evidence	113
21.	Murder Weapon	116
22.	Framed	124
23.	One Crime Solved	131
24.	Shocking News	135
25.	Cold Case	138
26.	A Haunting Truth	143
27.	And the Killer is …	149
28.	Bait and Lure	153
29.	Mystery Guest	156
30.	Seasoned Detective	160
31.	The Question He Needed to Ask	166
32.	Friends Together	169
33.	Old Lady Vibes	172
34.	Old Lady Fetish	175
35.	The Vital Clue	182
36.	The Horrifying Truth	192
37.	Dead End	196
38.	Aftermath	202
39.	Authors Note	205
40.	What's next for Patricia?	207
41.	Other Series by Steve Higgs	209
42.	Felicity Philips Investigates	211

43.	Pets Investigate	213
44.	Free Books and More	214
About the Author		216

Prologue - The Cake

"Oh. My. God!" Barbie squealed and bounced on the spot.

I'm used to my young friend's exuberance, but this was a level beyond the norm.

Jermaine thrust out an arm, his eyes going wide. "Is that ..."

Barbie let out a small scream. "Yes!"

Utterly lost, I asked, "Who?" My question referred not only to who were they talking about, but also who it was among the people pressing to come aboard the ship they had just spotted.

"Oh, Patty, you really need to read up on your celebrity gossip," laughed Barbie. "That's Stewart Dapples, the chat show host."

I blinked. "Stewart Dapples?"

"You must have heard of him."

I hadn't, but my lack of knowledge was not the thing bothering me.

"His name is Stewart Dapples?"

"Yes," said Jermaine and Barbie at the same time.

"Stu Dapples?"

Barbie and Jermaine were standing either side of me. They looked inward at each other, their eyes meeting as they tried to figure out what was tickling my brain.

After a moment, Barbie asked, "Why are you saying his name like that?"

Was it just me? "Stu Dapples?" I took a step back so I could look at them both at the same time. "Come on! Stewed apples! His name is 'stewed apples'."

Barbie and Jermaine looked at each other again. They had no clue what I was talking about. Maybe it was the way I was saying it or perhaps I was the only one who could hear it. The man had a ridiculous name and I doubted it would be the last one I was going to hear today.

I gave up and went back to watching the crowd of people on the dock outside.

My name is Patricia Fisher. I'm employed by Purple Star Cruise Lines as a detective on board the star of their fleet. I'm fifty-three, a good few pounds heavier than I might want to be, yet happy in my body, and I'm dating the captain of the ship. Alistair Huntley is handsome, never married, childless, a couple of years older than me, and an absolute dreamboat. I might have mentioned that he is good looking already, but it bears repeating.

I have a benefactor in the form of one of the world's richest men. The Maharaja of Zangrabar considered himself and indeed his country to be permanently in my debt – a story for another time – and due to that fact, he paid for ... well, everything.

Jermaine is my butler. He's Jamaican but speaks with an English accent he perfected by watching Downton Abbey. However, calling him my butler is a little misleading because he is so much more than that. He's my protector for a start. A skilled martial artist, I have witnessed him flatten a room full of men who might wish me harm. I love him dearly and would happily have him by my side as a companion. Yet he loves his role as a butler and trained hard to achieve what he believes to be a lofty post.

FOUR EX-WIVES AND A WEDDING

Barbie is a gym instructor from California. At twenty-two her body is a flawless example of what God had planned when he first designed 'woman'. Her breasts defy gravity, her blonde hair flows and moves like she's on a shampoo advertisement, and she is so ridiculously fit it makes me want to drop things on her feet to slow her down just a little. She has a slight limp at the moment from one of our recent adventures and can still move faster than me.

The pair of them choose to help me in my investigative duties because they find it exciting to do so. They are not wrong, though I guess that depends on one's definition of 'exciting'. If by the use of that word you mean getting shot at, chased, generally threatened and wondering if you will live to see another day then, yes, being around me is exciting.

We were standing at the edge of deck eight in a spot looking out over the quayside. It afforded the best view of the people outside as they funnelled into the ship. Docked in Miami for the last two nights, we were due to leave shortly in just over two hours. By then the ship would have hundreds if not more than a thousand new arrivals, many of which were aboard for a wedding.

A billionaire's wedding.

A wedding that had me on edge.

Not for any tangible reason, but because trouble seems to follow me, and I expected the inrush of celebrities and rich people to result in drama. It's my job to fix the drama.

My radio crackled. "Lieutenant Bhukari for Mrs Fisher, over."

I swore inside my head. Barbie and Jermaine heard the call, but were too distracted by whoever it was they had just spotted to look my way when I rummaged in my handbag for the infernal communications device.

"Deepa, it's Patricia," I replied. I'm supposed to stick with rank and names, but it seems like a lot of unnecessary formality and effort.

"Mrs Fisher can you come to the Charles Suite, please?"

A tic by my right eye twitched. Betty Ross, the bride-to-be was staying in the Charles Suite. There could be no good reason for anyone to want me to go there unless something terrible had happened. At least she wasn't dead; I would have received a coded message if that were the case.

Barbie heard me say I was on my way and was looking at me when I finished stuffing the radio away.

"You want us to come, Patty?"

I shook my head. "I'm sure it's nothing," I lied, fervently hoping it might be true for once. "You guys have fun spotting celebrities."

No sooner had the words left my mouth than Jermaine squealed and gasped. Barbie ran to the window. Walking away, my pace quick but not running, I heard them getting excited about someone called 'The Mouth'.

Wondering who or what such a person might be famous for, I put celebrities from my mind and hurried onward.

My dachshunds, Anna and Georgie, a mother and daughter duo who live with me on the ship and go more or less everywhere with me, led the way, trundling along with their little legs a perpetual blur beneath their sausage-shaped bodies.

They had no idea where it was we needed to go, but they dragged me along with an insistent hurry to get there, nevertheless.

Ten minutes later, I got a second call to check I was coming. I didn't bother to answer on the radio, opting instead to knock on the door, which I had just arrived outside, and use my universal keycard to enter the suite.

"Hello," I cooed, stepping over the threshold.

Inside the suite I found three of my team: Lieutenants Deepa Bhukari and Schneider, and Ensign Molly Lawrie. Schneider has a first name but no one ever uses it. Schneider is a tall Austrian, his hair currently cut into a flat top to make him look like *Ivan Drago* from *Rocky IV*. Deepa hails from Pakistan where she was an infantry soldier and sniper before she became a security officer for the cruise line. She has elegance and grace in her movements and skin kissed by the sun. Molly used to be my maid. The decision to join the crew came about when I brought her on board and her eyes were opened. She's a shade over five feet tall, with light brown hair and a petite figure.

They are all part of my team, assigned to work with me as I try to crack crimes occurring on board where the maritime laws and international waters make jurisdiction about as complex as it can get.

They were in the suite's central space looking at what appeared to be a cake on a table. Also in the room, a paramedic, the sight of which made my heart rate spike. Before I could speak, Tulisa Oswald, the groom's granddaughter, one of them at least, emerged from the toilet.

I wasn't sure how to address Tulisa as the last time I had any meaningful interaction with the teenager, it was to expose that she was stealing from her family to sell jewels and other easily shifted goods to subsidise her lifestyle.

She met my eyes and quickly looked away.

The toilet flushed, the familiar noise preceding Betty's appearance. Betty Ross is twenty-two like Barbie, but where my Californian friend is athletic, Betty is voluptuous. Blonde hair with loose curls fell below her shoulders framing a face that was not too dissimilar to Marilyn Monroe's.

Quite how the attraction to her eighty-two-year-old groom came about, I cannot say, but it didn't seem to be the money that did it.

She came out of the toilet looking gaunt and drawn, her face white and a hand over her mouth. The other paramedic – it was rare not to find them as a pair – was on her shoulder.

Anna and Georgie wagged their tails, happy to see everyone.

"Okay," I encouraged, the comment aimed at my team, "spill."

Deepa spoke for the rest of them. "Threatening message in a cake that was mysteriously delivered to Miss Ross."

Betty lowered herself into a chair. "Someone tried to poison me."

"I'm sorry, what?" The two things didn't match.

"Possibly poisoned," Kareshma the paramedic argued.

Before my confusion could deepen any further Molly jumped in with an explanation.

"The note in the cake says it is poisoned, Mrs Fisher."

Betty jumped to her feet and ran from the room again. Unpleasant noises ensued, the bathroom door still open so we all got to hear the bride-to-be emptying her stomach.

"Impulse reaction," explained Kareshma. "Probably."

Deepa said, "The cake will need to be tested. Miss Ross has no temperature and no symptoms to suggest she might have ingested a toxin."

"Like what?" I sought clarification.

Kareshma's partner, Adriano, a Polish man in his forties, rattled off a list, "Dizziness, disorientation, trouble breathing, faintness … the only box Miss Ross ticks right now is vomiting, and we believe that is a reaction to stress not her stomach rejecting what she ate."

"The doctor …" I started to say.

"Is on his way," Deepa assured me.

Betty's voice wailed from the bathroom, "I feel terrible. Who would do this to me?"

Tulisa hustled back into the bathroom to help her … her what? Let's see, Betty was marrying Tulisa's grandfather, so did that make her a step-grandmother? There was less than three years age difference between them.

Regardless, Tulisa went to help Betty and I crossed the room to see the cake.

"You said there is a note? Too much to hope someone signed it."

Deepa shot me a grin and pumped her eyebrows. "Way too hopeful." With a twist, she indicated a small bag on the table next to the cake. It had frosting stuck to the outside and finger tracks where someone – Betty, I guessed – had tried to wipe it off. "This was inside the cake. Rolled up so it didn't make too big a target."

"The note was already in the bag?"

"I guess whoever put it there wanted to make sure it could be read. We haven't taken it out yet. I doubt there will be prints on the bag, but we've been as careful as possible handling it so far. The cake was delivered," Deepa paused to check her watch, "just over an hour ago. Miss Ross says it was delivered by a steward. A Caucasian man in his mid-twenties with a tan."

"Well that narrows it down," I grumbled. Roughly half the crew are Caucasian, and more than half are men. The ship spent the last six weeks in tropical climes so every last one of them had a tan.

The note was flat on the table inside the small bag – a standard clip-top sandwich bag one could buy in almost any convenience store world-wide.

'*Go through with the ceremony and you will <u>die</u>. Enjoy the poisoned cake!*'

Betty was due to marry John Oswald on the top deck of the ship in two days' time when it sailed into New York past the Statue of Liberty. The note didn't contain a lot of grey area. It was typed in what looked to be font twenty, the last word of the first sentence underlined for emphasis as if any were needed.

There was silence in the room while I read the note, punctuated, rather unfortunately, by Betty heaving on her now empty stomach.

I straightened once more, pulling my lips to one side as I gave thought to what I needed to do next.

A knock at the door gave me a start and I twirled around to find Dr Hideki Nakamura coming through it, a bag in his hand and a rushed expression on his face.

"Heart attack on deck nine," he explained. "Patient came on board an hour ago and hadn't even made it to his cabin. His wife was giving him hell for ruining their holiday and threatening to stay on board without him. Took three security officers to calm her down so I could treat him."

"He's alive?"

"He'll be fine with some rest, but he's not going on a cruise today. Good thing it happened now and not tomorrow. Where's the patient?"

Molly showed Hideki to the bathroom just as Betty was leaving it again. He took her to her bedroom where she could lie down.

The bride's health was not a matter I could control – my job was to figure out who might want to scupper the wedding. A little voice at the back of my head wanted to point a finger at Tulisa, the groom's petulant granddaughter, but I couldn't do that without some evidence.

Dispatching Molly, Deepa, and Schneider in different directions with a singular task: find out who delivered the cake, I set off to see the groom.

Quayside Queue

The Miami sun beat down onto the quayside next to the giant cruise ship. Passengers due to disembark in Florida had done so when it arrived, clearing the way for new passengers to arrive.

Among the throng of those lining the dock was a middle-aged woman and her teenage niece. The woman came from Italian heritage, which gave her lustrous black hair that showed the grey if she didn't dye it, and hair on her forearms that she used to bleach when she was younger. Short and petite, Felicity Philips, a celebrity wedding planner, looked quite unlike her niece who inherited much of her father's genetic code.

Taller and broader, Mindy viewed the world, and especially boys, with scepticism. Trained in martial arts, she was rarely to be found without a weapon about her person. Leaving them behind to take the trip was a compromise she accepted though – what could possibly happen on a cruise ship?

"It feels weird to not have Amber and Buster with us," said Mindy, her head tilted back and her hands shielding her eyes as she stared up to take in the enormous structure of the cruise ship. The nineteen-year-old woman was in total awe. It wasn't that she had never travelled, but this was her first time on a cruise ship and seeing it in a brochure did nothing to prepare her for the sheer magnitude when dwarfed by its shadow.

Felicity had been trying hard not to think about her pets. "They will be perfectly well looked after by Philippe for the week that we are away." Her reply masked the doubt she felt about entrusting her most precious and precocious pets to her other assistant. The young man's life was something of a drama at the best of times and he could be so easily distracted.

"Well, it wasn't like we could leave them with Mum," remarked Mindy in a sort of absentminded way. She was about to board the luxurious cruise ship and could barely contain her excitement at all the wonder and extravagance she had to look forward to over the next two days. She was in Miami and would soon be in New York. Her friends at home were green with envy and so they should be.

Unfortunately, she was here for work and knew her time on board would be dominated by unavoidable tasks she would need to run between just to get them all done.

Felicity's lips tightened at the mention of her sister, Mindy's mum. Ginny had recently split from her husband, a situation Felicity hoped would soon be resolved and not just because she now had her sister and Mindy staying in her spare rooms.

It was a worry for another day. Another day when she did not have a billionaire's wedding to organise in less than two days without any of her usual support staff and on board a ship of all things. The guest list read like a celebrity who's who, but this was what she did. It was how she earned the big bucks and had a reputation as the person you could go to if you were rich or famous and needed your nuptials meticulously managed.

"Get off! Mum! He's 'ing doin' it again!" Felicity glanced to her left and tried not to frown. A British family were queuing rowdily a few yards away, making a lot of noise and augmenting almost every sentence with a selection box of expletives. There was a man there who might be the father to some of the unruly brood, but surely not all. He wasn't doing anything to manage them either way.

Also present, but too busy smoking cigarettes, were two women in their late forties. On the plus side of plus size, for which they could be forgiven, it was their dress sense and garishly coloured hair that wrinkled Felicity's nose.

Mindy huffed an annoyed breath. "Do you think they are in the right place, Auntie? They don't look or sound like they should be going through the royal suite's entrance."

It was a classist thing to say, but Felicity had to agree. The family's clothes, cleanliness, demeanour, and literally everything about them screamed unemployed and unemployable. Maybe they were lottery winners, Felicity mused, hoping they could board soon and never see the unpleasantly loud family again.

The white-uniformed security officers managing the foot traffic at the royal suite's entrance were handsome men and women baring smiles as they greeted each new party. The minor hold up was due to a glut arriving at the same time. Most were celebrities, Mindy getting just as excited as Barbie and Jermaine when she spotted someone she knew from the TV and internet.

Baggage handlers appeared from the ship to collect the next pile of suitcases, crates, and more.

Felicity checked her watch but knew she had been waiting no more than a couple of minutes. Spotting a steward coming her way with a tray of what looked like mimosas, she hoped she wouldn't be called forward next.

Expecting Patricia to show her face, and wondering why she hadn't, Felicity recognised the captain when he exited the ship. That the other officers saluted him was a bit of a giveaway, but she had met him in England not so long ago.

Trying to catch his eye and failing, Felicity spotted another face she knew, that of Archibald Gunn, an oil tycoon with ties to the groom. It was a matter of professional pride that she knew the name and face of every guest at each wedding she managed. That was quite a task on most occasions. This time around, it had proven impossible.

Not due to the number of guests or because many were celebrities. No, the biggest challenge this time around proved to be the bride's family. They were not famous or rich, Felicity knew that much, but other than their names, she had no idea who they were.

Assuming the captain had come down to the quayside to greet someone in particular, Felicity was shocked when he made a beeline for the unpleasant family. It suggested they were significantly more important or well off than Felicity assumed. Chatting amiably, the handsome man escorted them under the awning and into the ship. Felicity couldn't hear what he was saying; he was too far away and the background hubbub of conversation, dockside machinery noises, and the squawk of seagulls overhead ensured words would remain private.

Expecting to be next inside, Felicity picked up her small suitcase, the one she'd used as carry-on baggage for the plane. The rest of her bags were stacked in a neat pile where they waited for the stewards to be available.

However, before the security guards could get to her, a smart, shiny limousine swung into view at the prow of the ship. It had gone around the queue to angle in toward the royal suite's entrance. It wasn't one of the cruise lines' limousines which were easy to spot with their Purple Star livery, but a sleek black thing oozing class.

Seeing it approach, two of the security guards moved to intercept. They looked set to stop it before it could reach the awning over the entrance, but that changed when the captain reappeared.

Again, Felicity didn't hear what was said, but the two men aiming to stop the limo fell into positions three yards apart so it could pass between them and stop.

The captain waited for the officer on his side to open the door. Felicity half wondered if the King of England was about to step out. Or the President of the US perhaps. It had to be someone important. Yet accepting the captain's hand and leaning in to air-kiss his cheek was a woman in dark sunglasses and a broad-brimmed orange hat.

Her left hand reached up to brush lightly against the captain's shoulder as their cheeks touched. Her right hand, Felicity almost choked, held what appeared to be a gin and tonic.

The captain walked her to the ship, talking once more, his hands getting involved as he explained something. With a cheery expression, he left her at the door, the woman vanishing inside to be swallowed by the shadows.

FOUR EX-WIVES AND A WEDDING

The car swept forward and this time when the captain looked around, he was searching the small crowd. Saying something to the officer running things at the royal suite's entrance, the captain had her send the officers out to appease the few people still waiting to board the ship and, to Felicity's great relief, angled his feet to greet her himself.

A broad smile creased his face.

Mindy made a sound like a bull scraping its hoof before a charge. "That is one fine looking older man. Don't suppose he's got a son on board somewhere, does he?"

Felicity's face showed no sign she heard her niece's comment, and was quiet when she replied with, "No, Mindy. He does not have any children."

The captain was close enough to hear them now, so she stepped forward, raising her right arm to meet his. "Alistair, so good to see you again."

"Likewise, Mrs Philips. Please accept my apologies for the delay. We have an unusual number of special guests today."

"And some skanky ones," Mindy muttered under her breath.

"Let me escort you inside." The captain led the way, a small team of stewards falling in behind to collect and haul the luggage.

They didn't notice, but the wedding planner and her niece were being watched. A man in an ill-fitting suit long since out of fashion and at least a size too big for him observed Felicity Philips vanish inside the ship. He knew who she was. He knew her niece too and Captain Alistair Huntley for that matter.

The security officers managing the last of the people boarding through the royal suite's entrance paid him no attention – there were hundreds of people on the dock, making him just another casual observer.

He had chosen to remain behind a barrier rope a few yards behind where the VIP guests were queuing. There it looked like he was waiting for someone or something. Travelling alone, no one on board was expecting him, though he felt certain he was going to deliver a surprise to the one person he was here to see: Patricia Fisher.

With Felicity Philips lost from sight, the scruffy man adjusted the wheels on his small suitcase and walked back to the main passenger entrance. His cabin was located on deck eight; the best his funds could afford. It would be sufficient for his needs.

Felicity and Mindy found out the reason behind the slow onboarding process when they got inside – there was an elevator to take them up through the ship and it could only hold a limited number of people. The lady with the gin and tonic was still waiting for it, her glass now empty.

The captain regaled them with details about the ship and what they could expect to find. He knew they would be busy with planning and organising the Oswald wedding, but hoped Felicity and Mindy might have time to enjoy some of the Aurelia's amenities.

When the elevator car arrived, the captain made his excuses and promised to see Felicity again soon; he had other duties to which he needed to attend.

Leaving them with an escort he said, "Just follow Lieutenant Kapoor, Mrs Philips. He will take you directly to your accommodation."

"Right this way, Mrs Philips," the tall, lean security officer invited. "Deck twenty?" he asked the lady with the empty gin and tonic glass.

She replied, "Yes, thank you, Ragit," impressing Felicity and showing she had to be some kind of regular or long-term guest on board the ship.

"Here let me take that."

The lady handed over her empty glass which Lieutenant Kapoor handed to a steward before the doors swished shut with a whisper.

He pressed only one button: number 20.

"We're on the top deck too?" asked Mindy.

Felicity nodded, "It's where all the royal suites are."

Exiting the elevator into sunlight that stung their eyes after the artificial light in the enclosed steel box, Felicity and Mindy got their first proper look at the ship. Seeing it from outside was one thing. From the dock the Aurelia stretched into the sky like a building laid sideways. Inside where the private royal suite's elevator exited onto the top deck, passengers were treated to a view down the length of the ship.

The woman in the orange hat, her right hand now devoid of a gin glass, had seen it all before. She turned left upon leaving the elevator and strode around the corner out of sight.

Mindy gawped open mouthed at what looked like a floating city.

Just ahead of where they stood a hole plunged several decks through the ship. Escalators linked multiple decks which were festooned with shops and restaurants, arcades, spas, clubs, and all manner of entertainment venue.

"It ... it's just so big," Mindy stuttered. "How often do passengers get lost?"

Lieutenant Kapoor said, "All the time when they first come on board. There are lots of signposts to help people, but not enough it would seem. They orientate themselves soon enough though. You're staying with Mrs Fisher, yes?"

"Indeed we are. We're old friends," Felicity explained.

Mindy ran to catch up now that her aunt was moving again. "Do you know her?"

Lieutenant Kapoor sniggered at her question. "Mrs Fisher is famous around the world, not just on this ship. Everyone knows her."

Mindy conceded the man had a point and was about to ask how much farther it was when he stopped.

Knocking politely on the door with the knuckles of his right hand, the lieutenant stepped back a pace to wait.

Ten seconds later, the door opened, Jermaine filling the opening with his broad shoulders.

"Jermaine!" squeaked Mindy, unable to contain her excitement.

The butler nodded his head with a smile. Bedecked in full butler's livery complete with white gloves, he was not able to respond with such exaggerated excitement.

"Mrs Philips, Miss Walters, please come inside. Mrs Fisher will join you shortly."

"She's not here?" Felicity asked, confused as she went through the royal suite's small lobby to reach the masterful living space beyond.

Mindy whistled a noise of appreciation as she followed her aunt inside.

"Wow. Just wow. Patricia sure knows how to live. I would live on a cruise ship if my cabin looked like this."

"Impressive, isn't it?" asked a voice that made both women swing around to see who was there.

Surprised to find themselves face to face with the gin and tonic lady, it was Felicity who recovered first.

"Felicity Philips," she crossed the cabin, her hand extended. "You must be a friend of Patricia's."

The woman was two inches shorter having ditched her heels and was now without sunglasses, sun hat, or earrings. Better able to get a good look at her, Felicity figured they had to be about the same age – just the wrong side of fifty-five.

She gripped Felicity's hand firmly but briefly.

Jermaine, always on hand, stepped in to perform the introduction.

"Mrs Philips, I have the honour to name Lady Mary Bostihill-Swank."

Felicity blinked, the name rebounding inside her head. "Lady Mary? I ..."

"We met some years ago, my dear," Lady Mary replied with a smile, making her way around Felicity to head for the kitchen. "Don't worry, it was long enough ago there's no reason why you would remember me. It was at a wedding inside Claridge's. I was only there because Rod Stewart was attending and I wanted to hear him sing."

Mindy whispered, "Who's Rod Stewart?"

Ignoring her niece, Felicity followed after Lady Mary who had the refrigerator door open already and was rummaging inside.

"Gin, Madam?" Jermaine enquired.

"Yes, dear." Lady Mary closed the door, a bottle of Hendricks held triumphantly in her hand. She handed it over to the butler. "I'll let you make them, dear. You're so much better at it than anyone else."

"More gin?" remarked Mindy, her voice not quite quiet enough.

"Sorry, this is my niece, Mindy," Felicity explained. "She's also my assistant." Felicity did not add, '*Who should know better than to speak when she hasn't thought through what she is going to say.*' Instead she shot Mindy a look that drew a cheeky grin.

"So where is Mrs Fisher?" asked the teenager.

"That is the question," replied Lady Mary, her attention entirely on Jermaine's hands and the task they were performing. "No doubt engaged in shady business somewhere, tracking down a miscreant or looking for clues."

The Ex-wives

"Mrs Fisher, please do come in," invited Bartholomew, the butler in the Platinum Suite. His words came with a wry smile and amidst a barrage of shouted insults from inside John Oswald's cabin.

I pulled a face and peered around the butler.

"What's happening in there?"

"The former Mrs Oswalds showed up, Mrs Fisher. I feel perhaps Mr Oswald ought to have denied them entry."

"The former Mrs Oswalds?" I tried the term out for myself. "How many of them are there?" John had been married before, I knew that much. His first wife was a famous actress and with her he produced his son, Tim, who was on the cruise with his father. I wasn't aware of any other wives and it's not the sort of thing a person asks, in the run up to a wedding.

"Three so far, Mrs Fisher, though I fear the fourth might not be too far away."

I strode past Barty and into the suite where I found three women, all older than me, in various stages of wagging their fingers at John. Anna and Georgie wanted to be off the lead to explore and I was forced to tug them back to keep them from running amok. The familiar rumble of the ship's engines started, a faint noise most wouldn't even notice.

"She's just after the money, John," snapped a woman with flaming red hair.

"And don't tell us the pre-nup will protect your fortune, John, because it won't," fired the brunette next to her. "I found a way around it. So will she."

The third woman wore her hair naturally, the only one of the women, all of whom were in their sixties and seventies, with any grey. I guessed the original shade to be jet black, but there was little of it left now.

She was a little calmer than the other two when she said, "You are making a public spectacle of yourself, John. It's embarrassing to see you with a girl who is young enough to be your great granddaughter. Can you not see that?"

John Oswald had his arms folded across his chest in a casual manner and a genuinely amused expression on his face.

"Did the three of you rehearse this? Or am I witnessing the improv show? Where's Lexington, anyway? Did the three of you leave her out for a reason?"

I knew who Lexington Brand was. The blonde bombshell won three Oscars in the seventies and eighties and was John's first wife. She quit acting only a few short years ago and I could recall reading headlines stating she'd become impossible to work with.

Conspicuously absent, I questioned why John would have invited his ex-wives to his wedding. The kids, I assumed. He couldn't invite one without the other, though to my knowledge all his children were adults now.

The ex-wives were upset about his impending marriage and I kind of understood their viewpoint. However, if I was looking for someone who might want to threaten or poison John's bride, then these three were at the front of the suspects list.

The redhead was sucking in some air to launch her next offensive, so I got in first.

"Who sent the threatening note to the bride?" I asked, my voice loud enough to halt the argument. Outright accusing people isn't my style; I prefer to watch and assess so I know I have the right person before I strike, but my question suited the situation.

The three women and John froze, their heads snapping around to look my way.

Seizing the initiative before anyone else could speak, I stormed across the room to speak with John.

"There is a doctor with her, John. I don't think there is any reason to worry, but she is very upset." Explaining more fully, I said, "A cake was delivered to her suite on the eighteenth deck an hour ago. Hidden in the layers was a note stating the cake had been poisoned and warning Betty that she would die if she went through with the ceremony." John's face was one of horror quickly turning to anger. However, he didn't waste time shouting at his ex-wives, he ran to get his phone.

While he called Betty, I wheeled around to face his ex-wives, I asked, "Which one of you sent it and what was in it?"

The denials were instant.

"How dare you?" screeched the one with the grey hair. "I would never stoop so low!"

The redhead yelled, "That's a ridiculous accusation."

The brunette looked hot under the collar. Was it guilt I could see?

"None of us would poison the poor girl. We're here to stop John from making a mistake, but we're not killers."

It was the redhead who finally asked, "Who are you anyway?" Looking at the other ex-wives, she asked, "Who is she?"

I didn't have to answer, the brunette spoke for me. "She's Patricia Fisher. Aren't you?"

I nodded. "Yes, I am. I'm the detective on board this ship and I have a crime to solve."

"Well it wasn't us," snapped the redhead. The other two were calmer now, but she was as fiery as her hair. "I don't care who you are. Accuse me again and you'll be hearing from my lawyers."

I let her threat go without comment, turning my attention to John because it cut the ex-wives off mid-argument, and I wanted to see what they would do now.

John was in his bedroom, sitting on the edge of the bed. His phone was pressed to his left ear and his right hand cradled his forehead.

"I'm coming now," he spoke into the phone. "I'll be there as soon as I can. Patricia Fisher will catch the person behind this." He ended the call, pushing off the bed to get back to his feet. Already in his eighties, he looked to have aged a decade in the last five minutes. "Was it one of them?" he asked.

"Your ex-wives? They deny it, but I will find out. That much I can assure you."

"I must go to Betty. She says the doctor has given her the all-clear, but she's very upset by the note. Is it possible to arrange security to be with her until after the ceremony? I can pay the additional costs."

"Security will not be a problem." I should have thought of it already, but it was easily corrected. I would assign Deepa and Molly, the two female security officers to stick close by Betty's side. One of them could bunk with her for the next two days. I suspected it was overkill and there was no real danger to the bride, but it was only until the happy couple disembarked the ship in New York.

John took a light jacket from a closet, putting it on as he left his bedroom. I had gone out ahead of him to find the three ex-wives with their heads together. Their voices were low, and I got a furtive glance from the brunette. They were conspiring and doing little to hide it.

"Was it one of you?" John demanded, his voice harsh and angry. "Was it you, Carol?"

The one with the grey hair identified herself when she replied, "It most certainly was not!"

She made it sound true, but I wasn't convinced the ex-wives were innocent.

"How about you, Fiona?" John addressed the brunette, but she never got to deny her involvement. A rap at the door came before she could.

My dogs barked, as they always do whenever anyone knocks on a door, and I shushed them so I could listen to what was being said.

"Thank you all for visiting, ladies. It was nice to be reminded how torturous it was to be married to each of you. Now get out."

Goodness.

They were harsh words, but I might have much the same to say to my ex-husband, Charlie, if he chose to voice his opinion on my life or my choices.

The ladies were not inclined to leave and the finger wagging returned along with a rehash of earlier argument topics. Most went along the lines of making a fool of himself, that Betty was a little gold digger, and that they were not going to allow John to squander or risk their children's inheritance.

John just wanted to get to Betty, but everything changed when Bartholomew opened the door.

The person outside entered the room like she owned it and probably the entire ship. Lexington Brand was no longer young, but the vibrancy and beauty that put her on the big screen was still there. Dressed to kill in four inch heels and a fitted dress that must have cost a small fortune, she removed her sunglasses and levelled her glare at John.

"No."

It was a simple word that carried a truckload of meaning.

Expecting John to shoot her down with a loaded response, I was shocked to hear the timidity in his voice.

"What do you mean 'no', Lexie?"

"No, John. Exactly what I just said. You are not marrying that girl and that's the end of it." Lexington looked me up and down, decided I wasn't worth bothering with and aimed her 'drop dead' stare at the other ex-wives. "What are you crows doing here? Come to pick over a carcass, have you?"

Lexington clearly didn't care who she insulted. As the first Mrs John Oswald one of the other ex-wives present had replaced her and I questioned what the circumstances of that might have been. Was John cheating on Lexington at the time?

Hoping there would be no reason for me to need to find out, I thought I was going to find myself in the middle of a cat fight when the redhead snarled her response.

"Ha! The old 'has been' finally shows her face. You're a fine one to talk about picking over carcasses. Here to leverage some more money out of John, are you?"

Lexington took it in her stride. "If I choose to, yes. And better a 'has been' than a 'never was', Imelda. You were an actress for all of two minutes."

I had no idea what was going on, but Lexington had crossed the cabin, still acting as if she owned it, and was pouring brandy from a decanter. Having delivered an instruction to her former husband, it was as though the task was complete and the matter settled.

The redhead was being held back by Carol and Fiona. She continued to fling murderous insults at the tall, statuesque blonde woman as the butler did his best to remain dignified in the act of kicking them out. I remained quiet, curious to know what John was going to say next.

"Hey, John, fifth time's a charm!" cheered a man's voice, raucously. It came from the door and twisting around to look I discovered a man in his late twenties hanging through it. He had a tiny camera, one of those GoPro things, in his right hand. He stood well over six feet tall and wore a bright yellow suit with a black shirt, tie, and shoes. His hair was bleached almost white and teased into a series of spikes.

Bartholomew was doing his utmost to politely instruct the passenger to go away and getting completely ignored as though he were not even there.

"I have nothing to say to you," replied John.

"Ooh, look at all these ex-wives, John," the man continued unabated. "Will you ever learn?"

Just behind the young man was a woman with jet black hair. She was younger still and bore a figure that showed she spent a lot of time in the gym. She had a camera in her hands, filming through the doorway to the people inside.

Turning the camera back to capture his own face, the young man spoke to it, "That's right, folks at home. It's another exclusive from The Mouth, reporting live from the top deck of the Aurelia, an overpriced, first class rust bucket of a cruise ship if ever one sailed."

I gasped at his outright lie.

"Stick with me because there will be celebrity shenanigans aplenty as they gather for John Oswald's wedding to absolutely no one. Twisting his camera to face Lexington, The Mouth said, "That's right, folks. John has gone from an Oscar winning actress, who is looking especially haggard today, to total nobody. You could find a better match at your local seven eleven," he cackled into the camera, pretending he was a comedy genius and fooling nobody.

Lexington spat fury in his direction, but The Mouth simply laughed at her. Pushing away from the doorframe with a flick of his shoulder, the awful man continued talking as he went in search of his next victim.

Silence reigned for a few seconds, replaced by John once again insisting his ex-wives leave. That didn't extend to Lexington who clearly wasn't going anywhere.

When Carol, Fiona, and Imelda were gone, and the butler had once again retreated, he turned to face his first wife.

"Now, Lexie, be reasonable ..."

"I am being reasonable, John." She turned to face him, a brandy glass cupped in her right hand where her skin would warm the liquid inside. "I've been reasonable for forty years.

However, I'm done being tolerant. Unless you want people to know how you made your fortune ..."

John gave me a worried glance, checking to see if I was listening.

"Lexie, please," he begged.

She sipped her brandy. "It's a no, John. You will not degrade my lifestyle and that of my children and grandchildren any further by allowing that ... child," she clearly held Betty in low esteem, "to erode your fortune."

"She's already signed a pre-nup!" John protested.

"So did the others, John. It's not about her leaving you and taking half your money, it's about how much she will spend while you are married and about the impact on the firm's stock value. You're in your eighties, you old fool! How long are you going to live? What mess will there be when you die, and she announces she is pregnant? You won't be the first octogenarian to father a child. I'm not here to discuss it, John. The answer is a 'no'."

John was shaking with rage, but he wasn't arguing.

"You can't do this, Lexie."

"Yes, I can, John. We both know I can ruin you. The business and my interests will survive the fallout, but you won't."

"Neither will Tim. You would destroy your own son?"

What on earth were they talking about?

Lexie shrugged. "Tim is a big boy. I told him to distance himself from you decades ago. Instead he took the job you were offering. What happens to him will be his own fault."

"He's my eldest son, Lexie. The heir to my empire. Of course I wanted him to sit at my right hand side and to take the helm from me when the time came."

Lexie took another sip. "You're off subject, John. I already said no to the wedding. It's not happening. Have a party if you like; you have all the guests here already, but you step one foot down the aisle and I will tell the world about …"

"Shhhh- shh-shhush," John's panicked reaction to Lexie offering to spill the beans on whatever it was made me more curious than ever. Whatever she held over him, it had to be juicy and powerful. "Okay, Lexie. Okay."

I couldn't believe my ears.

"Good." Lexington finished her drink and placed the empty glass back on the sideboard next to the decanter. Trapping her purse under her left arm, she spun on one heel and marched toward the door. "I shall stay on board to make sure, John. I'll let you break the news to your bride."

John's phone rang as Lexie swished out through the open door. Bartholomew closed it after her, leaving just John and me in the suite.

"It's Betty," he mumbled, his voice quiet and his eyes down. "How am I ever going to tell her?"

Surprise Guest

The quandary John faced was not one I could help him with. I pressed him to let me, but he wouldn't tell me why he had to say yes to Lexington's demands. He didn't say much of anything, other than to reveal he couldn't tell me much of anything.

He ambled off to see Betty, his heart very obviously heavy with the burden of news he held, and I was left wondering what to do. The cake, though Dr Nakamura had been good enough to confirm the only poisonous thing about it was the awful note hidden inside, still required investigation. The minor problem with that was, however much I told myself to keep an open mind, I felt certain the ex-wives were behind it.

I needed to liaise with my team of security officers, but the first task on my list was to return to my own suite. There I expected to find Felicity and her niece. They had flown from the UK to organise the wedding which now looked to be called off. Someone had to tell her, and it might as well be me.

"Come along, girls," I encouraged Anna and Georgie to head in the right direction, angling out through a door to walk them along the sundeck.

The sun was high in the sky, though starting to dip and a light breeze ruffed my hair. The high rise buildings of Miami stretched into the distance, shimmering in the heat though I knew it was cool for Florida. Coming into winter, it was my second trip to the sunshine state and this time I had been in a better frame of mind to explore.

Upon arrival Alistair had a car waiting to take me down into the Keys where we swam with dolphins and drank cocktails watching street performers in Mallory Square. Located right on the waterfront, we kissed as the sun sank into the ocean. It was a perfect moment that ended all too soon. Thankfully, I would be back in a few months to do it again, the Aurelia's permanent journey around the globe ensuring it returned to many destinations over and over again.

Passengers were all around me, most paying no attention to the woman walking her dachshunds though I spotted a few who thought they recognised who I was. Recent events in my life have brought me a kind of infamy, but it is the ship that gets people to figure out who I am. I am known as a sleuth and my face has been splashed across the papers. However, the stories are all about me solving crimes on the ship. Or rather, one crime in particular.

My thoughts strayed to the Godmother and whether she would ever seek revenge against me. It was possible. Likely even, one might think. The fact that she hadn't, came down to me managing to topple her entire organisation in one fell swoop – there wasn't anyone left to send after me.

Arriving outside the door to my suite – the Windsor Suite, the finest the Aurelia could boast and mine in perpetuity due to the Maharaja of Zangrabar who paid for it and almost everything else in my life – I realised I'd been wandering aimlessly for twenty minutes, my feet guiding themselves as my mind drifted from thought to thought.

With a swipe of my doorcard, I let myself in. Jermaine, as always, appeared half a second later.

"Good afternoon, madam. You have three guests: Mrs Philips, Miss Walters, and Lady Mary Bostihill-Swank. They are in the kitchen with refreshments."

"Lady Mary?" I questioned.

Jermaine took the dog leads from me and my jacket.

"Yes, madam. You were not expecting her?"

"No, sweetie. I don't like to spring surprises on you." Had I known my English socialite friend was coming, I would have asked Jermaine to fetch several extra bottles of gin.

"Patricia!" she hallooed cheerily when I emerged from the lobby and came into sight. "Surprise!"

"Hello, everyone. It's so nice to see you all. I trust your journeys were relaxing." My remark was aimed more at Felicity and Mindy than Lady Mary who would have been in first class if not in a private jet. The woman had money. Serious money. It was old money too, the kind that never seems to run out and doesn't get spent so much as it gets invested. She owns a zoo for a start, and I know that pulls in a wad of money every year.

Felicity and Lady Mary were on their feet, standing so I could greet them both in turn. We air-kissed as old friends do, and I got a wave from Mindy who was good enough to put down her phone.

"Did I miss something?" I asked Lady Mary. "Did you tell me you were going to be on board?"

"Goodness, no, darling," Lady Mary scooped her current gin and tonic from the kitchen's long breakfast bar. "It's all so last minute. I'm here for John Oswald's wedding. We both contribute to several of the same charities and met years ago. It might have been the eighties. That decade is something of a blur."

That she knew John was news to me, but wasn't that great of a shock. Lady Mary knew lots of people. Politicians, royalty, celebrities ... name a person and there was a distinct chance my gin-sozzled friend knew them directly or by connection to someone else.

"Ah, about the wedding," I said.

Felicity read my face.

"What about it?" she begged for me to spill the beans.

"Well, it might be off."

Mindy punched the air. "Woo-hoo!" Two days of cruising!" She leapt off her barstool. "I'm getting into my bikini! Where's the nearest pool?"

Felicity held up a hand to slow her niece down. "Not so fast. When the people paying for it say it's off, then it's off. Until then we have a lot to do. Even if it is called off, we still have a lot to do because we will have to cancel the flowers, caterers, event organisers, the guy with the thousand doves they plan to release, the chap bringing the swans ... there will be deposits to reclaim where possible ..."

Mindy accepted defeat, slumping grumpily back onto the stool.

"We won't need to start straight away though, so if you want to take an hour ..."

Mindy sprinted across the suite, vanishing into one of the bedrooms where we heard a suitcase open a nanosecond later.

"Might I fix you a beverage, madam?" asked Jermaine. He'd taken up position in the kitchen where he had already cleared away the plates from lunch. He was asking if I wanted a gin and tonic, but I declined the offer.

"Tea, please." The whole thing with John was bugging me and I felt on edge. Gin might have helped to calm me, but would also blunt my brain.

As it was, I didn't get anything to drink because my radio crackled.

"Secretary, secretary, secretary. Mrs Fisher to the elevators opposite the Mardi Gras club on deck nineteen." The person sending the message, almost certainly a member of the ship's security detail, repeated it through once more.

I lifted the radio to my lips and pressed the send button. "This is Mrs Fisher. On my way. Out."

Lowering my arm again with a sense of dread creeping up my spine, I nearly jumped when Felicity spoke.

"What did all that secretary stuff mean? Was that code?"

"Yes," I nodded grimly. "Someone just found a dead passenger."

Murder

Lieutenant Commander Martin Baker was there by the time I arrived. He's the ranking officer in my little team and not half bad as an investigator. Married to Lieutenant Deepa Bhukari, the Irishman was on a career path to the top.

I'd chosen to leave the dogs behind – a crime scene isn't really the place for them – but had Lady Mary and Felicity in tow.

Lady Mary's husband is a thriller writer, so to her a murder was just fuel for his next book. It had to be murder too; I would not have been summoned for an accident or a heart attack. Felicity, I knew, was no stranger to drama in her own life – a recent run of mysterious events and a few deaths at weddings she arranged had forced her to turn sleuth more than once.

They were accompanying me out of natural curiosity and the belief they were going to get drawn into helping me solve the case.

Martin came away from the elevator when he saw me approaching. There were officers positioned in the passageway to keep people back and turn them away. They would apologise and give them an alternate route to reach their destination. There were more officers blocking the view into the elevator. Two of them were members of my team: Ensign Sam Chalk and Lieutenant Anders Pippin.

Sam used to be my assistant when I had (briefly) my own private investigation business in England. His mum's older sister was in my class at school and I remember him being born. He's thirty-one, about five feet nine inches tall and has Down's Syndrome. He's a member of the crew and assigned to me. He does everything the other security officers do, but he isn't cleared to carry a weapon – his cognitive reasoning just isn't up to it. Nevertheless, he is an asset to my team for his ability to see things from an angle no one else would ever consider.

Anders is South African, slight of build, and still in his very early twenties.

Their bodies blocked the view, which I was glad about though I knew I would have to take a look soon enough.

Martin said, "There's no identification on the passenger, Patricia." It had taken me a long time to convince the team to call me by my first name. It was how I addressed them. "It shouldn't take us long to figure out who she is though."

"Murdered?" I enquired straight to the point.

Martin nodded, his face grim. "Stabbed in the back. Looks like a single wound. The killer struck and ran would be my guess and he or she took the murder weapon with them."

"Who found her?"

"A young couple on their honeymoon. They only just got on and were heading for a bar. They were rather shaken up by it. I've made the captain aware. I expect he'll meet with them personally later."

That was likely. Alistair looked after his passengers in such a manner that he made them all feel like the cruise ship was built and operated specifically in the hope they might come aboard.

Hearing my voice, Sam turned around to give me a wave and a goofy grin.

"Hello, Mrs Fisher." He was still in the habit of addressing me formally and I wasn't going to push him to stop. Sam moved his feet when he turned around to give me a wave and in so doing exposed the body in the elevator.

I jolted.

"That's Lexington Brand," I breathed.

Lady Mary rushed to my shoulder to see for herself. "How can you tell?"

The victim was lying on her side facing into the elevator so there was no way to see her face. The blonde hair, dyed that way, but looking natural and multi-tonal, covered her face even if she had been facing outwards.

I didn't need to see the face to know who it was. The dress and shoes gave her away.

My voice quiet and my mind racing, I said, "I met her earlier. She's John Oswald's first wife."

My revelation wasn't news to Lady Mary who knew all about John's ex-wives and claimed to have met Lexington at a party in New York in 1985 or thereabouts. It was at the height of the actress's fame, and she'd just won her third Oscar.

Felicity stayed back; she had no desire to see the body.

Lady Mary murmured, "I guess Lexie finally pushed her luck too far."

I had to know what that remark meant.

"Well," Lady Mary picked her way around what she wanted to say. "She was known for telling people precisely what she thought of them. It made her a lot of enemies over the years. She was manipulative too."

"I thought you were friends?" Felicity voiced her confusion as she came nearer.

"Oh, I never said that, sweetie. I knew her, but I wouldn't stay in the same room as her if I could help it. The woman was pure poison."

I huffed out a hard breath, agitated as I so often am at the start of a new investigation. Murder automatically carries a greater burden: it must be solved and quickly to boot. A pickpocket would need to be dealt with, but the two crimes do not compare.

"I need to find John Oswald." It was a blunt statement. My mind chose to race, thoughts and ideas battling with a growing to do list.

Lady Mary frowned. "You don't think John did this, surely?"

I took a moment to explain what I had not already told them: that it was Lexington who stopped the wedding. She had something she could hold over John and less than half an hour after her grand entrance, she was dead.

John had everything to gain by taking his first wife out of the equation. At the very least, I would have to eliminate him from my enquiries.

Felicity sighed. "Wedding or no wedding? I wonder which it will be."

What she wasn't saying, I suspected, was how difficult a task it was to organise the whole thing in two days. That two days was being eroded fast by uncertainty and if it were to go ahead, what might the mood be in the wake of a murder?

At least Lexington wasn't on the guest list.

"Ooh-hoo-hoo, what do we have here?" the raucous voice I now recognised as belonging to The Mouth echoed in the passageway.

Martin was already moving to intercept the grinning form who was angling his camera to get a shot of Lexington's body.

He gasped, "Is that Lexington Brand? Hey, folks, here's the scoop of the week: it looks like Lexington Brand, former Oscar winning actress from the eighties has met a sticky end on this floating dung pile of a cruise ship."

Security officers had raced to Martin's aide, pushing The Mouth back by blocking off the passageway with their bodies and walking forward.

The Mouth raised his camera high to keep filming.

"On this rust bucket of death, the only question I have is, whose chest do we pin the medal on."

His voice faded as the security team forced him away from the body.

"Who was that awful man?" asked Lady Mary.

I explained in brief terms and giving myself a mental shake, I gathered my thoughts. Martin positioned officers to prevent anyone else getting close and was on his way back when I sprang into action.

"Martin, I need the team to get cracking."

He was all ears.

"Please have Molly stick to Betty Ross like glue. She needs to move into her suite and go everywhere with her. I will be asking Betty to stay in her suite as much as she can. Make sure Molly is armed. The threat to the bride might be legitimate or bogus. Until we know for sure, we must operate as if her life is in jeopardy. I'm sure dealing with the body is already in hand, so I'll not involve myself in that. An autopsy report, even if it's a cursory one, as soon as the doctors can manage, please. We need to be certain about the cause of death and anything they can tell us about the weapon used will be helpful."

Martin made notes on his tablet and a yard away, Lieutenant Pippin was on the radio making arrangements.

"I'm going to track down John Oswald. Please circulate his picture to all security officers and have them looking for him. In fact ..." I paused to take out my phone. I was supposed to use the radio, but the same channel is used by all the security officers, and I hate always having to use formal radio speech.

When my call was answered, I said, "Molly, it's Patricia."

There was a beat of silence before Molly said, "Yeah, it tells me that on my phone when you call."

FOUR EX-WIVES AND A WEDDING

I couldn't tell if she was being sarcastic or just trying to explain how phones work. I let it pass.

"Is Mr Oswald there? You are still in Betty's suite, right?"

"Yes, I'm still here. Anders just told me I should stay here and keep a close eye on Miss Ross. Mr Oswald isn't here though. Is he supposed to be?"

Yes, I thought to myself. He left his suite to go to hers. That he failed to arrive did not bode well.

"Sit tight. Try to convince Betty to stay there. I'll be along as soon as I can." I ended the call quickly and turned my attention back to Martin. "We have a killer on board. If it's not John Oswald, and I'm kinda hoping it isn't, then we need to figure out who it is quickly."

It was an obvious thing to say, but no less true for it.

"I'm going to see Miss Ross," I continued. "Can you please find out where John's other ex-wives are staying …"

Martin interrupted me, "He invited his ex-wives?"

"No, I don't think so. I think they are here to mess with the wedding."

"That sounds about right," groaned Felicity.

"Now that one of them is dead, I need to speak with them. Martin, find them. Let's get them interviewed. In the few hours since they came on board, we've had one death threat and one murder. I don't plan to wait to see what happens next."

With that, Martin made sure Anders and Sam had all they needed, then hurried away – he had jobs to do.

"What can we do to help, sweetie?" asked Lady Mary. "I can scope out all the bars on this deck if you like. I bet John is in one of those. That's where I would go if I'd just murdered someone."

It's where Lady Mary would go no matter what she had just done, but I didn't say that. Instead, I encouraged her to do precisely as she suggested. Maybe John *was* in a bar. I wasn't going to allow myself to assume he was guilty just because he had every reason to kill Lexington. If he was completely innocent, there could be a dozen reasons why he didn't go straight to Betty's suite to break the news about their wedding. Building up Dutch courage might be one of them.

Turning to Felicity, I asked, "The rehearsal dinner is due to take place tonight with a whole bunch of VIP guests. You have that all in hand?"

Felicity pulled a face. "Hardly. I mean, assuming it still goes ahead, I know most of the arrangements have been made, but I haven't confirmed anything with my own eyes. It's what I ought to be doing now."

"You should go ahead," I replied, then in a change of plans said, "In fact, I'll come with you."

Felicity and I bustled away, our feet aimed for the prow of the ship where the big banquet hall could be found. Normally the ship's upper deck restaurant, it was the best space to be converted into a function room and boasted panoramic views of the ocean on both sides.

Lady Mary went in the opposite direction, bumping into a man who didn't see her because his attention was on the two ladies now heading away. He apologised and they both sidestepped, creating a moment of awkwardness as they chose to go the same way and once again blocked the other person's path.

"I'll stay still. You go," said Lady Mary, tutting in her head at the man's scruffy clothes. His belt was old and frayed, the leather around the buckle flaking off. It made him look like he'd recently lost a lot of weight.

The man muttered another apology and his thanks, but the woman he was trying to catch - Patricia Fisher - was already gone.

Shoplifters

Heading across the ship on our way to the top deck restaurant where the rehearsal dinner would take place tonight and then the wedding breakfast in two days' time, I heard my name echoing out of my handbag again.

"Lieutenant Chadwick to Mrs Fisher, come in, over." He had to say the message three times before I managed to get the wretched device up to my mouth and press the button to respond.

"Mrs Fisher, over."

"Mrs Fisher, are you available to attend *Top Brands Boutique* on deck eighteen? It's a rather sensitive matter."

"We are talking about a crime that needs investigating, right? I'm kind of in the middle of one already."

There was a brief pause before Chadwick's voice came back. "Yes, Mrs Fisher. It will be easier to explain when you get here. Chadwick out."

Felicity caught me muttering under my breath.

"You have quite the demanding work life," she observed.

"Some days," I had to admit. "Other times there is nothing much going on and I get to relax and sunbathe."

"Oh, that sounds nice. Cruising around the world to exotic locations with nothing much to do."

The truth was that I got significantly less downtime than I thought I ought to. Considering the cruise ship as a microcosm of society, the crime rate is shockingly high. Most especially when one takes into account the average age of the cruise ship traveller is north of sixty.

It didn't help that I had an ongoing mystery that started with the body of a stowaway. Found in the hold with a knife still in his chest, Finn Murphy was an enigma demanding exploration. He had uncut gemstones in his belly and when we found where he'd been sleeping – in a storeroom way down in the bowels of the ship – his knapsack was full to the brim with priceless and rare gold coins and yet more jewels.

I knew the haul to be worth millions and could guess that it was what resulted in his murder. The killer, whoever that was, failed to find the treasure, but I believed what Finn Murphy held was likely the tip of the iceberg.

Our research to date led us to Rio where Professor Noriega just happened to be the world's leading authority on a Spanish ship called the San José. It sank hundreds of years ago filled with treasure plundered from South America.

Or did it?

That was indeed the question and one I felt we needed to answer if we were ever to solve the riddle of Finn Murphy's murder. That is, after all, my job: to solve crimes committed on board the Aurelia.

That Professor Noriega was murdered weeks before we arrived in Rio, and a man posing as the professor came on board the Aurelia to talk to me about the dead stowaway, deepened my belief that we were standing on the cusp of a major historical find. A find that would be worth billions at today's rates.

Barbie was doing what she could to figure out what we could do next, but the trail went cold in Rio and the treasure we recovered from Finn Murphy was stolen by an unnamed thug who broke in at night. The enormous man proceeded to beat up Alistair and Jermaine before diving over the side of the ship. He tried to take me with him and almost succeeded. Goodness knows what might have become of me if I had not been able to escape.

Thoughts surrounding that mystery swam around my head on the way down to deck eighteen.

To my knowledge I had never been inside Top Brands Boutique; it wasn't a shop selling the kind of clothes I might choose to wear. Aimed at under thirties, it specialised in high fashion casual wear which is to say they sold really expensive sweatpants and hoodies.

I could hear the commotion below from the escalator as it descended from deck nineteen. The white uniforms were easy to pick out, but I was surprised to see so many of them. Expecting Lieutenant Chadwick and maybe a partner, I counted no less than ten security officers attempting to contain the situation.

"Get out of my 'ing way!" screeched a woman. Though I could not yet see her, the voice came laced with information. She was neither young nor old – in her late forties, I guessed. She was English and from the south somewhere; an area of low means and income. The final part I surmised from the number of expletives employed and the way she dropped the H, T, K and several other consonants from her words. A nineteen letter alphabet might be more expedient, but for the sake of communication it was doing her no favours. Mind you, I say expletives, but all she actually ever said was, 'ing'. It's an odd word to employ in my opinion.

"Get off my 'ing mum!" yelled a teenage boy, employing the same odd, abridged expletive as his mother.

Coming closer, I saw him lunge to strike at the arm of a security officer who was doing his best to keep the loud woman in place.

There were other voices, all bearing the same terrible, guttural accent and from a mix of ages. Some were adults, but most were children.

"She said she didn't 'ing steal it!" shouted another woman. "We're not 'ing thieves!"

"You just left the store with an unpaid for item in your bag!" claimed a new voice, this one belonging to the shop assistant I guessed - it had an Australian twang to it.

Unfortunately, her reply caused a fresh barrage of abuse.

"You'll be 'ing hearing from the 'ing captain about this!" threatened the first woman; the one I took to be at the centre of the drama. "You'd better let me go now or there will be 'ing consequences. You'll all be out of your 'ing jobs!"

Closing in, I could see what appeared to be a family. The team of security officers had managed to corral them to one side in between premises where they surrounded them in a loose circle. Just outside the circle stood two members of crew. They were shop assistants employed by the franchise, not the ship, but had to qualify as crew all the same. They wore name badges to show who they were.

The family were dressed in what, for the most part, looked to be hand-me-down or charity shop clothes and were easily identifiable as a family by their similar features and shape. The woman at the centre of what I assumed was a simple case of shoplifting – we don't get a lot of it, but it happens – had a shock of blue hair, but not in a good way.

If Barbie dyed her hair blue, it would look cute and she would accentuate it with her choice of makeup and clothes. The lady to my front had dyed her hair to escape the grey creeping in and her clothes and makeup choices made her look deranged. Not least for the bright green sweater she wore.

The focus of the group was on a different item of apparel, a black hooded top being held by Lieutenant Chadwick. It had the legend 'Hood Babe' across the chest and looked exactly like the one displayed in the window of the shop from which the lady had undoubtedly been attempting to steal it.

"Oh, Lord," said Felicity, hustling along by my side. "I saw them on the dock. Alistair came to greet them in person. They are as common as muck." I hate to judge people and I know Felicity is much like me in that. However, breeding, income, and circumstance aside, one doesn't require those things to be a decent person.

Observing the event from the deck above, the man in the ill-fitting suit chose to remain where he was. He could go down to Patricia Fisher right now, but he was in no rush, and he had just spotted something – he wasn't the only one watching her.

And that changed things.

Finally arriving – I'd jogged across the wide mezzanine floor from the escalator but avoided running so I wouldn't be out of breath when I got there - the security officers saw me coming and looked only too pleased to turn the situation over.

"What seems to be the problem?" I asked, my tone polite as I spoke to Lieutenant Chadwick and then shifted my eyes to look directly at the woman with the blue hair. "Hello, I'm Patricia Fisher, the ship's detective. I'm sure we can get this all straightened out with minimal fuss. Why don't you tell me what's going on here?"

"What's going on? What's 'ing going on?" she wasted no time in beginning to rant again.

"I shall ask you to refrain from using profanity in public. There are children within earshot."

"Don't I 'ing know it," she replied, huffing. "Most of 'em are 'ing mine."

She really was about as unpleasant as I could imagine a person being.

"They accused me of stealing!" she arrowed a hand at the two ladies from the boutique. "Me! Why would I steal? My daughter's marrying a 'ing billionaire for crying out loud!"

"Yeah!" echoed more than one of her family.

Inside my head, I chose to 'ing swear myself.

I had no idea who these people were until that moment, but with the dots connected, I realised I'd spoken to the woman before.

"Mrs Helen Ross?"

Her next words died in her mouth as her brow furrowed in question.

The woman to her left, a sister, I felt certain, asked, "Here, 'owd you know that?"

I kept my eyes on Betty's mother.

"We spoke on the phone. Do you remember?"

I saw recognition dawn in her eyes.

"Oh, yeah. You called about my Betty. So you're gonna get these goons to 'ing leave me alone now, are you? I haven't stolen nuffing," she reiterated a point I felt certain was a lie.

"Of course, Mrs Ross. Such a terrible misunderstanding." I could hear whispers passing between the security officers around me and the two shop assistants who were being more vocal.

"That's more like it," said Helen's sister, nudging her. "This 'ing billionaire lifestyle's summit I could get used to."

Turning to the shop assistants, I asked, "Did either of you observe Mrs Ross handling the garment in the shop?"

They looked at each other, their wide eyes making it clear they could not believe I was questioning their claim of shoplifting.

"Sorry, ladies. I need an answer."

"Well, no," said Erica, the one with the Australian accent. "But that's …"

I cut her off. "How did you find the garment? If you didn't see her take it off the rail or shelf, how did you know she had it?" I expected to hear she set off the alarm since I know the high price items are fitted with tags the staff remove at the till. I was not to be disappointed, but things were not so clear cut.

"It was lying on top of her bag!" scoffed Erica. "I mean, it was so blatant. Then the alarm went off and she acted all surprised."

"That's because I 'ing was!" growled Helen.

I sucked in a breath and held it. I could probably make life uncomfortable for Mrs Ross, but even though I felt certain she was guilty, the most I could realistically do was eject Helen and her family at the next port where they were disembarking anyway.

Speaking quietly to the shop assistants, I explained what was going to happen. They didn't exactly like it, but they understood.

Facing Lieutenant Chadwick once more, I said, "Let's disperse the surplus officers, please. There's no need to keep them from their duties any longer."

"What about this?" Chadwick held up the 'Hood Babe' hoody.

"Return it to the shop?" I suggested, one eyebrow raised to make him think for himself.

The Ross family were getting ready to leave the area too, the lot of them grumbling and griping with far more volume than was acceptable.

Stepping into Helen's path, I met her eyes and lowered my voice.

"You are here for your daughter's wedding, Mrs Ross. Please keep that in mind and try not to embarrass her. I trust there will be no further incidents where shop assistants mistakenly accuse you or anyone in your family of shoplifting?"

She narrowed her eyes at me in warning and came a step closer.

"I said I didn't 'ing steal it. It wasn't even my size."

"Be that as it may, Mrs Ross, I would hate for there to be reason for me to have anyone confined to their cabin. Can I ask that you check your bag next time you are leaving a shop. It would be most unfortunate for there to be a second item mistakenly placed there."

If she could burn my face with her glare, I would be on fire. However, sensing I wasn't going to let her go until I was satisfied, she mumbled, "Yes."

"Then you have two days to enjoy yourselves. I trust you will experience all the Aurelia has to offer."

She didn't reply, except to ask, "Can we go now?" The question came with attitude and a sense of threat.

I nodded to the security officers who were still hanging around. They spread and I watched as the bride's mother waddled away with her family, the lot of them complaining and whining as they shot hate-filled glares over their shoulders.

Once they were out of earshot, Felicity said, "They are really not very nice. I wonder what the groom will make of his new in laws."

I had no response worth voicing.

The situation dealt with, Felicity and I set off once more, aiming for the banquet hall on the top deck.

We didn't get there on our second attempt either.

Interview

The call that diverted our route came from Lieutenant Deepa Bhukari. John Oswald had been found and there was fresh blood on the cuff of his shirt.

He claimed to have no idea where it had come from. Deepa was wise enough to wait for me and had taken John to an interview room on deck ten. There my team has an area set aside for our investigations. We have room to store equipment, interview rooms should we need to grill suspects or more gently coax the truth from victims, and space where we can analyse what we know or spitball ideas.

We don't have any cells though. If it is necessary to confine a person for their own safety or that of others, and their cabin proves not to be an appropriate space, they can be taken to the brig. It is down in the bowels of the ship, several decks below the passenger levels.

There was no need to involve Felicity any further – our initial intention was to get her to the banquet room so she could organise the rehearsal dinner, so I gave her directions and sent her on her way. Whether the dinner or even the wedding went ahead was a matter for debate, and one I hoped to resolve shortly.

Arriving at our rooms on deck ten, I found Lieutenant Schneider just inside the door. He had his hat on and was about to leave.

"There's something happening in one of the bars," he explained. "It's The Mouth. He's been assaulted."

"That does not surprise me." The words just slipped from my mouth, and I closed it guiltily.

Schneider looked at me with a raised eyebrow, paused half in and half out the door.

"Sorry. I met him earlier. He's vile."

"Hard to imagine he has many friends when all he does all day is find bad things to say about anyone with the slightest claim to being a celebrity. The bigger they are, the harder he goes after them."

"But he's popular on the internet?"

"Goodness, yes. His online shows are growing in popularity. I guess it's one of the advantages of the internet – he gets to livestream himself causing embarrassment to celebrities. If someone is looking at someone else's wife or boyfriend or whatever, he will catch them. If they are committing dodgy tax businesses, he will expose them."

I shrugged. "It sounds like people are safe if they are behaving themselves."

"You would think that, but if celebrities have nothing dodgy going on, he just makes it up."

"How can he get away with that?"

Schneider chuckled. "He doesn't. He gets sued constantly, but that just makes him more famous which brings more people to watch his shows and that makes him rich enough to risk getting sued. It's self-sustaining."

I marvelled at the concept, but let Schneider go. The security team on board are there to react if there is a fight or someone is doing something they ought not to be. However, for the most part they are window dressing and spend their time making sure people can find their way around the giant ship or helping little old ladies with their sun loungers and parasols.

The investigation stuff comes down to my team.

Deepa had John Oswald sitting at a table inside an interview room. She was outside waiting for me.

Reporting before we went in, she said, "He seems genuinely confused about why I asked him to come here." Trebor and Cuttherage found him in the Pearl Bar on deck sixteen."

"Deck sixteen?" I repeated, questioning if I heard right. "That's in the opposite direction to where he was supposed to be going."

"And not far from the elevator bank where Lexington Brand was found." Deepa made a pertinent point.

"What has he said so far?"

"Only that he needed time to think about what he was going to say to Miss Ross. I asked him how the blood got onto his shirt – Trebor spotted it – but Mr Oswald maintains that he had no idea."

That was enough information for now. I gripped the door handle and let myself in, hoping I wasn't going to find the groom was guilty of murder.

"Patricia, why am I here?" John asked, rising to his feet the moment I came through the door. "And why did I have to hand over my shirt like it's evidence or something? What's going on?"

I waved for him to sit.

"Lexington Brand is dead, John." I used the news like a bat to whack him over the head. I wanted to see how he would react. Would he be shocked? Would he try and fail to fake his shock because he already knew? Would I be able to tell if he was faking?

His eyes flared, his brain processing my statement.

Then he closed his eyes, bowed his head, and leaning forward he made fists, placing them both on the table as if they were needed to keep him upright.

With his head still bowed, he asked, "Is it really terrible that I am pleased?"

"That depends on whether you killed her, John."

His head snapped back up to see if I was serious. Seeing my expression, he started talking fast.

"You can't possibly believe I would kill her, Patricia."

"What does she … did she hold over you, John? She commanded you to stop the wedding and you agreed to do it. Some would see that as strong motivation to want her out of the picture."

John's lips flapped up and down before his next words found his voice. "Yes, but I would never kill her. You have to believe that."

"Whose blood is on your shirt, John?"

"I have no idea. I think perhaps I should speak to my lawyers, Patricia. I had nothing to do with Lexie's death, however it happened, and I'm not the kind of person who tolerates being accused." He was becoming defensive, the shock (if there ever was any) of Lexington's death passing quickly.

I had no doubt what he said about his tolerance levels was true. A person doesn't get to make billions unless they are capable of dominating their environment.

John started toward the door, making as if he was simply going to leave. I stepped in his way.

"John, I'm tracking a killer. I need to know the extent of your involvement before I let you go. The demand for a lawyer doesn't hold the same level of threat here in international waters as it does on land. I can throw you in the brig if I deem it necessary." I wasn't about to do any such thing to an eighty-two-year-old man. "But I know that you and I can discuss this matter rationally," I added quickly, "so that I can be assured I am not letting a killer walk free." Dropping my voice to a tone that begged his assistance, I said, "I need your help to find the person behind this, John."

His full head of righteousness wilted a little. It made me think he wasn't to blame, which was a relief.

"I want to speak with Betty," he replied. "Does she know?"

"That one of your ex-wives was murdered today? Not from me. Following the threat in the cake, I tasked an armed member of the ship's security team to remain in Betty's cabin until I find out who was behind it. I doubt your fiancée will have heard anything."

He nodded his head thoughtfully. "I was on my way to tell her I couldn't go through with the ceremony when I got cold feet. That's not a feeling I am used to, you understand?"

"Why head to deck sixteen, John? What's in the Pearl Bar that drew you so far off course?" I wasn't really asking why he went there, though I was curious. Rather, I was coming at the question of its proximity to the murder from an angle.

I got a one shoulder shrug, a gesture that suggested he didn't know how to answer.

"I wasn't heading anywhere really. On my way to find Betty, I ran into some wedding guests and that got me feeling off balance. They were shaking my hand and saying kind words while I was on my way to stop the event. So I got on an escalator. I wanted a drink, and I knew the bars on the top decks would be filled with people who would know me. I couldn't very well drink my sorrows away while wedding guests congratulate me."

His explanation held water.

"I couldn't have told you the name of the place I went into. I could smell the liquor, so in I went."

"How much did you have?"

"None. I was still nursing a bourbon on the rocks when two of the security chaps found me."

Deepa confirmed what he was saying with a nod.

Accepting what he'd told me so far, I pushed to know more.

"John, I need to know what Lexie was using against you …"

"No." He said it with purpose and zero room to manoeuvre "I will not discuss that, Patricia. Not under any circumstances. Lexington was an evil, manipulative woman who I should never have married. All you need to know is that I didn't kill her."

I went through John's timeline after leaving his suite to being found in the bar. There was a lot of it that could not be corroborated. He bumped into some people who knew him – wedding guests – and they might be able to give a rough indication of when that was. The bar staff in the Pearl Bar would be able to show the receipt for his drink and that would confirm what time he arrived. However, between those points, he had enough time to kill his ex-wife.

Did I think he had?

No.

However, I had to consider him a suspect.

When I explained that, it did not go down well.

"Patricia I am not going to be confined to my cabin like some common criminal. Maybe maritime law does rule out here on the waves, but I can assure you my lawyers will shred Purple Star within seconds of me calling them. I can buy the cruise line should I want to."

I wondered if that were true.

"I did not kill Lexie and I am getting married in two days' time. I have a rehearsal dinner tonight, so you either need to make good on your threat to throw me in the brig, or let me go free right now."

He was doing a good job of keeping a lid on what anyone could see was mounting frustration and anger. The gauntlet was down now though; his ultimatum delivered.

I let him stew for a second, tilting my head slightly to the left and eyeing him critically. I was making it look like I needed time to consider my options. Not because I needed any time to think. It came down to whether I truly believed John might be guilty and I didn't.

The blood on his shirt had yet to be explained and he possessed both motivation and opportunity. Over the course of the next few hours, my team and I would pull apart the evidence: the blood analysis, messages on Lexington's phone, timings, witness reports, and whatever else we could find.

On land, it would be a different story, but out here on the open ocean, John couldn't hide from me. He couldn't escape, though I would be sure to tell the bridge he wasn't permitted to use the helicopters or summon his own – a few of the high roller passengers came to and from the ship at sea like it was a daily commute.

Confident I could let the octogenarian go without endangering anyone, I ended my charade.

"Very well, John. I'm not prepared to lock you up. I've no wish to and I'll go so far as to admit that I pray you are as innocent as you seem."

"I am," he remarked, frowning as though it were obvious.

"However, it is only fair that I caution you. It is my duty to the cruise line, the ship, and most especially the passengers aboard it, that I keep an eye on you."

John narrowed his eyes. "You're giving me a chaperone?"

"Yes, John. Lieutenant Bhukari," Deepa dipped her head to make it clear it was her to which I was referring, "will accompany you until I can identify the real killer."

Scruffbag

The man in the ill-fitting suit saw when Patricia Fisher and Felicity Philips split to go separate ways. He had to flip a mental coin, but chose to follow neither. He expected Patricia to spot him if he got too close to her; she was an observant person, and he wasn't here to see Felicity.

He was on board the Aurelia for a secret purpose, one he had revealed to no one in the world. Patricia would find out soon enough and he might have tackled it head on had Felicity Philips not been waiting quayside to board the ship.

Curiosity drove him. It always had. There was something going on, that much was obvious, and he had a fairly good idea what it was for on his way to surprise Patricia Fisher in her suite, he'd heard a coded message carried on the airwaves.

He hadn't intended to hear it. A passing security officer's radio chose to squawk at precisely the right time. Knowing what it meant, and with the security officer dashing away, the scruffy man chose to follow.

What he believed to be the death of a passenger, most likely in suspicious circumstances given the request that Mrs Fisher attend, had the security officers scurrying here and there. He almost caught up to her at the crime scene, but bumped into one of her friends – another woman in her fifties. The well-spoken lady held him up, though it was not deliberate, and by the time he found Patricia again, she was attending to an incident outside a clothing shop.

About to descend on the escalator, he spotted someone else keenly watching the same gaggle of people with Patricia Fisher in the centre.

The other person, a man in his forties with good hair and a defined chin, used a pair of binoculars to better scrutinise what was occurring and there could be no doubt Patricia Fisher was his target.

Sooner or later, the scruffy man knew he would have to reveal himself. For now though, and largely because he wasn't the only person watching Patricia Fisher, he elected to observe.

When the man with the good hair set off again, the scruffy man watched with interest. He wasn't following Patricia at all. If anything, he was tracking Felicity. Scratching his chin, the scruffy man followed.

Some minutes later, Mrs Philips, an attractive woman in her fifties, walked into a large room clearly being set up to host a meal. Tables arranged to form a large circle would seat at least a hundred guests.

The observer had no idea what the event was, though he felt certain it was a wedding given the presence of such a prominent wedding planner. Assuming then that a wedding breakfast was due to take place following a ceremony, he shot his cuff to check his watch and turned his head to look out the windows.

It wasn't quite dark, but full sunset could only be a matter of minutes away. It seemed a strange time to get married, though he recalled reading about couples performing their nuptials under water or skydiving from a plane. Compared to such extreme examples, at night aboard a cruise ship could be considered pedestrian.

The man with the good hair had likewise tailed Felicity all the way to the banquet hall. He didn't stop, choosing instead to walk right by the doors. Only a single glance revealed his curiosity. The scruffy man now faced a choice – approach Felicity, explain why he was on board and see what she knew, or continue to track the man who was following her.

Deciding it was better for now if no one knew he was on board, he went with option B. If the man with the good hair noticed him talking to Felicity, it would erode the anonymity he currently possessed – a weapon that once squandered could never be regained.

Checking to be sure Felicity wasn't looking his way, he hurried by the open doors of the banquet hall. Scurrying after his mark, the scruffy man caught a sound that reminded him of trips to the dentist. He paused to listen, just for a second, but short on time, dismissed it
.

Risotto

"Good evening, madam," Jermaine greeted me as I came through the door.

The heads of both dachshunds popped up. They had been asleep on the sofa until that point and wore their faces sideways, their jowls stuck at odd angles as they bounced onto their paws and onto the carpet. Barking unnecessarily, they charged across the suite to get to me.

Dropping to one knee, I greeted them warmly. Both rolled onto their backs at my feet wanting their tummies tickled.

"A beverage, madam? Something to eat?" Jermaine was very good at making sure there was food ready to go. My days are a mite unpredictable, so while I try to plan meals, it often proves impossible.

I rose from the floor, the dogs flipping back onto their paws to follow me.

"Yes, to both, I think. Thank you, Jermaine. Perhaps a small gin and tonic?"

Jermaine inclined his head and went around me to return to the kitchen.

With a hand against the wall, I shucked my shoes. I don't wear tall heels; I find myself running far too often to even consider it, but I will wear a feminine shoe that gives me an extra couple of inches. Everyone else is so tall. Except Molly. Out of everyone in my immediate group, she was the only one shorter than me.

Leaving them placed side by side neatly in the lobby so Jermaine wouldn't feel he needed to make them tidy, I padded barefoot across the carpet with my dogs tracking along on either side.

"They are due their evening meal, madam, if you wish to provide it." Jermaine was such a sweetie. He knows I like to feed the girls.

They danced under my feet, getting in the way until I placed two small bowls under their noses. Their bowls were labelled with their names, not that they seemed to care. When I looked up, a goblet of gin and tonic, flush with ice and cucumber sat on a coaster inches from my hand. Condensation was beginning to form on the outside of the glass.

"Wild mushroom risotto, madam? Miss Berkeley requested it."

On cue, my gym instructor friend and part-time roommate appeared behind me. Wearing a towel and with wet hair, it was clear she'd just left the shower. Barbie splits her time between a room in my suite, because it is plush and yards from the gym where she works, and a double cabin on the crew decks where she cohabits with Dr Hideki Nakamura, her boyfriend.

"Hey, Patty, I thought I heard the dogs barking."

"Yes, please on the risotto," I let Jermaine know. Turning my attention to Barbie once I'd collected the now empty bowls, I asked, "How did the celebrity spotting go?"

Her eyes went like saucers filled with sparkling starlight. "Oh, my goodness! I got so many autographs! Didn't we, sweetie," she included Jermaine.

Jermaine looked a little embarrassed but admitted, "Yes, we did."

"Anyone I would know?"

Barbie's eyes flicked up and right as she engaged the memory portion of her brain. Holding up her right hand, she began to count off names.

"Well, there was Tom Hanks and his wife, I'm guessing you know him."

I shot her a frown.

She listed more than three dozen people, only two of whom I knew. She had selfies with most of them.

"I'm hoping to get a load more tonight and I need to see if I can find The Mouth."

"You mean at the rehearsal dinner? Is he on the guest list?" To my knowledge the dinner tonight was reserved for family and close friends.

Barbie shrugged. "No clue. But half the people at the wedding are famous so if they are going to be there, it's a fairly safe bet The Mouth will be too. He'll be filming for his podcast and next show."

"Or livestreaming the whole thing," remarked Jermaine.

Barbie gasped. "I could get on his show!" Her mouth hung open. "What should I wear?" I don't think the question was meant to attract an answer, but I gave her one anyway.

"Something that shows cleavage." When she raised one eyebrow, I added with a shrug, "If you want to get noticed."

Her frown deepened. "I get noticed for these," she made a show of staring at her boobs, "quite often enough, thank you." Smiling again, she said, "You're probably right though." She gasped again, a new thought pinging into existence. "Maybe I'll wear a dress, so I look like one of the attendees."

Virtually vibrating with excitement, she ran back to her bedroom to look through her wardrobe.

Jermaine called after her, "Dinner will be ten minutes."

I was glad to hear it and my stomach growled in protest. I needed to investigate the murder and liaise with the team about John's ex-wives and with Molly about Betty and the cake threat. I was invited to the rehearsal dinner as Alistair's partner and needed to get ready for that too. I wasn't going to make it to dinner in three hours without eating something now though and dinner would start with cocktails; the food would come later.

I sipped at my gin and thought about Lexington and John. There was no love lost between them that was for sure. He called her evil and manipulative, and she clearly held something over him. He had blood on the right cuff of his shirt, exactly where one might expect to find it if he stabbed his ex-wife in the back.

My head shook itself from side to side, an argument raging inside my head. I needed an answer on the blood.

Downing the last of my drink, I slid off my stool at the breakfast bar.

"When were the dogs last out?"

Jermaine looked up from the stove. "I planned to take them after I have served your dinner, madam."

"Super. I think I'll take them now. I need to check on something."

"You do not wish to wait for the risotto. It will be a few more minutes." He was apologising for the rice taking its sweet time to soften.

"Sorry, sweetie. Please plate it up and keep it warm. I'll be back soon."

The girls understood enough of the funny noises the humans made to know they were going out. I turned around to find them eagerly poised to run for the door. With a clap of my hands I got them moving. It was time to get some answers.

Saboteur

Mindy found the banquet hall only when a steward escorted her there. Her aunt started calling almost an hour ago, but she hadn't noticed at first because she was chatting with a boy. A man, she corrected inside her own head. At nineteen, she was single and free which was great in theory. It wasn't like she planned to find a husband and have kids any time soon.

She wasn't looking for casual sex either, but it was nice to have boys take an interest. Getting ignored when you are sunning yourself in a string bikini does nothing to a woman's confidence.

When finally she noticed the missed calls and text messages, the sun was setting and though it was still warm, the temperature had dipped noticeably in the last thirty minutes. She needed clothes and ideally a shower, so by the time she went looking for Aunt Felicity, she had more missed messages.

Perhaps she shouldn't have said she would be there shortly when she replied the first time.

Huffing a frustrated breath and muttering that her aunt was going to kill her, Mindy thanked the steward and hurried toward the banquet hall doors.

Mindy pressed her shoulder up against the righthand door and was about to shove it open when she spotted an old woman acting furtively. Inside the banquet hall, the grey-haired old lady was doing something and checking over her shoulders while she did it.

Her actions were blatant. Anyone seeing her would know she was up to something, but she was at the side of the room behind a screen that hid her from the other people in the room. Only someone entering would be able to spot what she was up to.

Mindy's phone beeped again with yet another incoming text message. Certain it was her aunt, she didn't even bother to look, but reached into the stretchy pocket on the hip of her sweatpants to flick the switch across to silent.

Standing outside the door, Mindy continued to stare through the round semicircle of window, her oblique angle not the best, yet all she had. Should she go inside and confront the old woman? The moment Mindy opened the door, she would react and stop what she was doing.

Mindy chose to watch for now, but took out her phone.

Someone had messed with the bride earlier today, she knew that much. It was how she got to spend more than an hour lazing by the pool. Mindy cursed herself for failing to pay attention when Mrs Fisher had explained what happened. Did she say something about an ex-wife?

I mean, Mindy would have listened and paid attention, but it was sooo boring. Especially when compared to sunning herself by the pool with a magazine. How many of her friends could claim to be doing the same?

None. That's how many.

The old woman took another glance over her shoulder, leaning out slightly to get a better look and twisting to check the doors.

Mindy ducked, dropping into a crouch and holding her breath. Had she been seen?

If the groom was in his eighties, then the grey-haired woman acting suspiciously was about the right age. She was too far away for Mindy to judge her age with any degree of certainty, but her grey hair and withered frame gave her cause to think she was well into her retirement years.

Levering herself slowly up to half height so she could peer through the bottom edge of the window once more, Mindy almost did a backflip when she saw the woman striding directly for her. She was leaving the banquet room and coming through the door by Mindy's head in the next second.

With no time to improvise, Mindy dropped to her hands and knees and closed one eye tight shut.

The door opened into her elbow, Mindy using it to protect her head.

"Oh," said the woman, surprised to find someone behind the door.

"Can you see a contact lens on the floor anywhere?" Mindy asked, looking up with her one eye shut as she patted the deck with open palms. "Stupid thing just popped out."

Now that she was close enough, Mindy could see she was right about the woman's age: mid-seventies or thereabouts. Ancient so far as she was concerned. Her aunt was ancient too for that matter. I mean ... fifties. How did anyone ever get that old?

With an expression that Mindy read as anxious, the woman made a sound of apology and hurried on her way.

Mindy waited, gritting her teeth while arguing what to do. Her gut said to check where the woman had been. Convinced she was up to no good, she wanted to see what nefarious deed she might have been completing. However, if she went to check inside the banquet hall the woman and her identity would be gone. On a ship this vast, would Mindy ever find her again?

Cursing that she hadn't used her phone to get video evidence, Mindy yanked it from her pocket and set off after the mysterious old lady.

She got precisely three feet. Then the door to the banquet hall opened and Felicity exited with a glare that could strip paint.

"This had better be good, Mindy. I realise this is a cruise ship and it's all wonderful and exciting, but you're not here on vacation."

"No time to explain." Mindy grabbed her aunt by the wrist and started moving. Significantly stronger, she had no trouble tugging the smaller woman along in her wake. "That woman was just in the banquet hall messing with something."

"What the … Hold on. What do you mean messing with something?"

"I'm not sure." Mindy let her aunt's wrist go but didn't stop moving. The old lady with the grey hair was forty yards ahead and about to turn a corner. She either hurried or ran the risk of losing her. "She was acting strange. Kept checking over her shoulder to make sure no one could see what she was doing. Any idea who she is?"

Felicity, mired in tasks she felt she had to do even though they were already done – she needed to check for her own sanity and peace of mind – wanted to get back to them. More than that, she wanted to delegate half to the assistant she brought with her. Okay, so everything appeared to be in order – the crew were as efficient as Patricia suggested – but it was her name behind it all. Her NAME. So, yes, she was going to double check everything was done the way she wanted it.

Now Mindy was saying she had a saboteur?

"What was she doing?" Felicity pressed. Then, remembering Mindy asked a question, she said, "I don't think she's a guest. I don't recognise her."

"Me either," said Mindy, pretending she had spent hours memorising the faces of all the guests attending like she knew her aunt always did. The truth was she'd spent more time doing it for this wedding than any previously. This wedding had an abundance of celebrities including some seriously famous and rich people from the world of film and music. Mindy would not mind meeting one or two of the single men from that pool.

"Where is she going?"

Mindy said, "That's what I'm hoping to find out. Want to give Mrs Fisher a call?"

Bloodwork

I was just about to go through the doors to sickbay when my phone rang. Expecting it to be a member of my team ... hoping might be more accurate, I was surprised to see Felicity's name displayed on my screen.

"Everything okay?" I asked.

Felicity made a noise that sounded like she was sucking on her teeth with indecision.

"Maybe," she replied hesitantly. "Mindy spotted someone doing something in the banquet hall."

I blinked and tried to decipher the message. Paused outside the door to sickbay, I knew the people inside would be able to hear me, so I popped my head around the edge of the door to mouth my need to take a call.

The dogs went through the gap the moment I created it, forcing an awkward dance with the door and their extendable leads to get them back into the passageway outside.

"Someone doing something," I repeated.

"Okay, I guess that's not exactly exact," sighed Felicity. "Mindy said she was acting strange."

"Suspicious." I heard Mindy's voice in the background. "Furtive. Definitely up to no good."

"And where are they now?"

"Um, ahead of us," revealed Felicity unhelpfully. "I'm not sure where we are, I'm afraid. We followed her from the banquet hall."

Finally a piece of information that told me something: we were dealing with a woman. A familiar itch at the back of my skull sparked a question.

"Is it one of John's ex-wives?"

"That I don't know," Felicity admitted. "It could be. I guess she's around the right age."

"Describe her."

"Um, five feet sixish. Grey hair. Mid-seventies."

"Carol." I couldn't know if it was her or not, but the description fit and if she really had been in the banquet hall doing something suspicious, I was willing to bet I had the right person.

"Knee-length blue floral dress and a string of pearls, plus a Versace handbag that matches her shoes?"

I could hear Felicity squinting at her phone.

"Sometimes you are really quite spooky, Patricia."

That was good enough to confirm I had the right person.

"You need to figure out where you are. There will be numbers on doors and if you come to an elevator bank, they are numbered too. There are crew everywhere. Grab the first one you can, tell them you are working with me and get them to accompany you. When Carol stops, have the crewmember find a member of the security team and then have them call me. Can you do that?"

"Can you send someone to check what she was doing in the banquet hall?" Felicity relayed Mindy's information which was sketchy at best, promised to do exactly as I asked, and got off the phone.

I then used it to call Lieutenant Commander Martin Baker. The team were all over the place, each of them assigned to be doing something. Martin reported that he had the cabin numbers in which the ex-wives were staying – all suites on deck nineteen, and that none of them were to be found there. He also let me know they had been unsuccessful in tracking down the steward who delivered the cake. Betty gave a good description but the cake hadn't been made in any of our kitchens which meant someone had brought it on board. It was that or someone baked it in their kitchen and only the best suites on decks nineteen and twenty had kitchens equipped for such a feat.

A little itch in my head knew that meant the man with the cake either wasn't a member of crew or they were but had been bought. I swung toward the former as the most likely scenario.

A threat inside a cake, a murder, and now someone allegedly messing with the preparations for tonight's rehearsal dinner. Were the ex-wives behind it all?

With Martin on his way to the banquet hall, I sucked in a deep and calming breath, held it for two seconds, then exhaled. Yeah, that did nothing for my heartrate which was high and climbing.

Shoulder barging my way through the door, the dachshunds threatening to trip me in their haste to go through first, I waved a hassled hello to the people on the other side.

Senior doctor on board, Dr David Davis, looked up from his computer.

"Good evening, Patricia. You are here about the blood found on the shirt cuff." It wasn't a question, and he was already rising to his feet. "I wish you had called ahead. I'm afraid the analysis isn't back yet."

I half expected that to be the case.

"How long do you think it will take?" I could see he was about to say something like, *"How long is a piece of string,"* so I rephrased my question. "Ballpark. Are we talking this evening or in the morning?"

He scratched his head. "Probably this evening," he hazarded, sounding not the least bit confident. "It's always hard to say. If we had the equipment on board …"

"Too expensive to be used as rarely as we would," I said so he wouldn't need to finish his sentence. The samples were taken here, and it was easy enough to match the blood types. However, unless we are talking about Rhesus Negative or some other rare blood, it was far too inaccurate to use as evidence. "Can you call me when you get the answer?"

"I will leave a note to make sure Dr Nakamura does precisely that. We are changing over shortly."

It was as good as I could hope for. My journey down through the ship to sickbay had been for more than just a question I could have asked over the phone – I wanted to give myself time to think for a start. The dogs needed the exercise too.

Thanking the doctor, I left him to his work and started back toward the elevators.

I was almost there when I got another call from Felicity.

Lies

Felicity was outside a suite on deck nineteen. With Mindy, she followed the saboteur all the way to her cabin and watched from behind the fronds of a large potted fern when Carol swiped her key card and went inside.

Somehow, they had gone all that way without bumping into a single member of crew. It seemed impossible, but I wasn't going to challenge her claim.

They found one shortly thereafter, a member of the security team no less. He confirmed their location and would have called me had Felicity not beaten him to it.

I called Jermaine on my way, arranging for him to collect the dogs. I loved having them with me, but I was going to be interviewing suspects shortly and it wasn't something I could do with a dachshund on my lap.

I had Baker and Schneider meet me in the passageway along from Carol's door. By then we had confirmed the cabin was assigned to Carol Oswald. She had remarried some years after divorcing John, but chose to keep his name. It struck me as odd, but maybe there was something in making sure John's children carried their father's name and not adopt their stepfather's. I could only guess and it had nothing to do with my investigation that I could see.

Forming a quick huddle with Felicity, Mindy, and Ensign Waddle, a newish member of the security team I recognised but was yet to ever speak to, Martin and Schneider revealed what they found in the banquet hall.

"Firecrackers?" Mindy jinked an eyebrow. "Really."

"On a remote switch," Martin pointed out. "Electronic fireworks have been around for years. They are safer and designed so folks setting fireworks off for celebrations at home don't have to be in the vicinity of the explosive when they are igniting them. You can buy them almost anywhere."

"They were right under a smoke alarm," explained Schneider, giving colour to the picture. "Set them off in the middle of the rehearsal dinner and not only do you have people screaming and running for cover because they think they are being attacked, but you set off the smoke alarms so the room would be evacuated."

Felicity looked like she wanted to boot Carol's door down.

"I am fed up with people trying to ruin my weddings," she growled through a clenched jaw. "Was there anything else? Any more booby traps?"

"Not that we could find," Martin did his best to reassure. "I think I should arrange to have a team sweep the place though. Lieutenant Schneider can supervise it all."

I patted Martin's arm. "Please do that, sweetie. In the meantime, we need to ask Mrs Oswald some rather pointed questions. Still no sign of the other two ex-wives?"

They shook their heads.

Felicity touched my arm just as I turned to follow Martin to Carol Oswald's suite.

"We really need to get back. The reception for the rehearsal dinner is due to start in an hour."

I could hear how hard she was trying to contain her rising panic. I sold her the concept of the wedding as an easy deal. The catering, decorating, venue and goodness knows what else would be managed by the crew - all she needed to do was tell them what to do and help John spend his money.

She had only been on board for a few hours and things kept going further and further sideways.

There was no reason for her to still be involved in what we were doing. Saying as much, I wished her luck with the event, offered a prayer it would go according to plan, and expressed my doubt that I would get there in time.

With Carol to interview and a ticking clock, I reluctantly sent Alistair a message explaining where I was and what I was doing. He would understand. In fact, as captain with a killer on board, he would probably rather I was sleuthing my way around the ship than joining him for dinner.

Martin was good enough to wait until I was ready. He'd collared Ensign Waddle since he was present and not on his way to perform a vital duty, so with them in front of me, Martin knocked, called out that he was entering and used his universal card to open the door.

As the door swung wide and the two men went in ahead of me, I saw why we couldn't find the other two ex-wives: they were in Carol's suite, the three of them thick as thieves.

Their shocked expressions, mouths hanging open and scarlet cheeks would have told me they were guilty if I didn't already know.

"How dare you!" snapped Imelda, her face beneath the flaming red hair filled with righteous indignation. "What right have you to enter this room unannounced and uninvited?"

Carol and Fiona took a second longer to rally but they were going to spit similar questions if I gave them a chance.

"Every right, actually," I replied calmly. I chose not to point out that we were in a cabin not a room. "You should study maritime law if you have any doubt. "I can enter your cabins and I can have all three of you thrown in the brig should I deem it necessary." It is rare that I have cause to speak to any passenger in the manner in which I was currently addressing John's three remaining ex-wives.

"You wouldn't dare!" Fiona insisted though she didn't sound entirely sure of herself and was too busy watching what Martin was doing to meet my eyes.

I was focused on Carol. She was the quietest of the three. Her eyes were also tracking Martin's movements as he laid the firecrackers out in a line on the coffee table.

"What are you doing? What's this?" demanded Imelda.

"Evidence." It was a simple statement. "Carol was witnessed placing these explosives in the banquet hall just a short while ago." Yes, I used the word 'explosives'. They explode, don't they? "Your desire to derail the wedding is not just failing ladies, it is landing you in hot water."

A muscle in Imelda's jaw twitched.

Carol looked positively sick.

They did not, however, crack.

"That's a blatant lie," scoffed Imelda. "Worse than that, it's slander. I want to know who made such an outrageous claim? Carol has been in her cabin with us for hours."

"That's right," said Carol, clutching at the lie like a drowning person grabbing hold of a floating branch. "I haven't been anywhere since … since I last saw you in John's suite," she embellished the lie, her words gaining in false confidence. "I came straight here, and the ladies joined me. We've been discussing the ridiculous situation we find ourselves in."

Fiona joined in. "John can't have more than a few years left. Why would he choose to make such a fool of himself with such a little gold digger."

"I blame Tim," said Imelda, the three women carrying on as if I and the security officers were not there.

"Yes," agreed Carol. "Tim should have put a stop to this nonsense the moment it started."

"Why did you kill Lexington?"

My question silenced the room. I watched their eyes, laying a personal bet it would be Fiona who cracked first.

I was wrong though. None of them did.

In fact, Carol frowned in deep confusion. "What are you talking about? Lexie's not dead. We spoke to her only a few hours ago."

Imelda voiced her thoughts, "That scabby old cow can't be dead; the sun would be shining and there would be a party if she was."

"Yes," I replied, "I noted your hatred for her earlier. Some might consider that motive."

Fiona's quiet voice asked, "She's really dead?"

"Yes. She was murdered not long after you all left John's suite."

Imelda smiled triumphantly. "Well that puts all three of us in the clear. We were together in a bar discussing John and his ridiculous need to remarry. I'm quite certain you can confirm that with the bar staff serving us."

"That's right," agreed Carol. "I haven't been anywhere near the banquet hall, wherever that is."

I was getting nowhere quizzing them like this. I needed to separate the ex-wives and attack their lies from new angles. That they were lying was in no doubt; I would believe Felicity over them any day of the week. The question I had was all to do with how deep their lies went.

A click from behind me announced someone new entering the suite. I had to twist at the waist and shuffle my feet to face that direction, but was looking the right way when it swung open.

FOUR EX-WIVES AND A WEDDING

"Meemaw, I was able to ..." he froze mid-sentence, his eyes filled with panic. He could have changed what he was going to say and finish his sentence, but I think he knew that I could see the guilt in his eyes.

Without another word, he bolted, dropping the to-go cup of soda so it splashed and leaked all over the deck.

Martin shouted, "Run!" his comment undoubtedly aimed at Ensign Waddle. They both took off, haring from the cabin at such a speed they had to grab the door frame to make the turn into the passageway.

Sighing, I turned to face the three ex-wives feeling very much outnumbered.

A little unnerved, I cracked a smile and said, "Don't you just hate it when they run."

Gate Crasher

Felicity tapped her fingers on the face of her wristwatch. It was a present from Archie, her late husband, and something she treasured even though it had little monetary worth.

Guests were beginning to arrive onto the sun terrace beyond the banquet hall where Captain Alistair Huntley mingled and chatted along with the bride and groom.

The posted time for dinner to commence was eight o'clock, but of course no one turned up on time. Certainly not celebrities who would often go to outrageous lengths to one up their peers.

That was the world in which she operated. It was stressful, pulling off the big events, Felicity's stomach knotting to the point where she thought it might burst on some occasions. Today was no exception and this was just a rehearsal dinner.

The security team arrived en masse and under Lieutenant Commander Baker's watchful eye, they quietly and carefully went over every inch of the banquet hall. It was clear of booby traps they assured her. Not a fork was out of place.

The chefs were hard at work, the stewards knew their jobs back to front and unlike the staff Felicity usually hired for her events back in England, the stewards on the ship acted as waitstaff to celebrities, rich people, and royalty every day.

FOUR EX-WIVES AND A WEDDING

It did little to calm her nerves.

One of the young commanders, a man called Mophuthing from Botswana, was the master of ceremonies for the night. He was confident and engaging when speaking to people and was outside now mingling with the crowd on the forward sun terrace where it was cool yet still warm depending where in the world a person hailed from.

Coming from England at this time of year it was practically boiling.

Mindy appeared to her aunt's right, running into the room from the kitchen where Felicity sent her to perform a third and final check of dish numbers. Mindy gave a thumbs up – the kitchen was good to go.

Stewards were moving through the guests, their trays of cocktails gratefully taken.

"It's all going to be just fine," Felicity told herself. "Nothing to worry about."

She got to regret her words an instant later when an outraged shriek rang out.

Outside on the sun terrace, which was still called that at night when it was lit only by the moon, Barbie was having the time of her life.

John Oswald knew so many famous people. In the last hour she'd learned that one of his side ventures was to finance movies. He'd started out with a low budget film about a fish by an unknown director called Steven Spielberg. That was in the mid-seventies and he'd met a lot of actors, directors and other movie people since.

Barbie counted no less than seven Oscar recipients in the first ten minutes.

Of course, she wasn't supposed to be at the party. She hadn't intended to gatecrash either. Hanging around outside where she hoped to catch a glimpse of a few famous people and maybe get some selfies for her social media profile, she waved to get rap star Death Pillow's attention. She wasn't expecting anything more than a photo opportunity, but he insisted she accompany him to the rehearsal dinner.

"Babe, my date refused to get on the boat. Said she is afraid it won't float. Now I have no date for the dinner and that ain't gonna make me look like a winner." He rapped his invite to an imaginary beat and held out his hand for her to take. "Come on, pretty lady, it's cool. Don't leave me hanging here like a fool."

Giggling through her nervousness and excitement, Barbie accepted the million-selling rapper's hand and let him lead her out to the sun terrace.

She had been on it a thousand times before, but it never looked like this on her previous visits. There were famous people in every direction and in between them were the seriously rich.

Whispering to herself, she repeated a mantra, "I love Hideki. I love Hideki."

Liam Hemsworth winked at her when she caught his eye.

"Dammit," she whined, "Why do I have to love Hideki." She was mostly joking. It wasn't like she was cheating on her boyfriend by attending a celebrity dinner. He was working anyway, and she would be sure to make it up to him when she got the chance. Unless Liam Hemsworth asked her to marry him. Obviously.

A party atmosphere filled the air, the bride and groom making a point to greet everyone in turn. There was no sense of the drama Patty mentioned earlier.

Until The Mouth showed up.

He wasn't invited but he also wasn't the kind of person who would let such a trivial detail get in his way.

"Hey!" he shouted, making sure people looked his way. "Look who we have here. Stepping out on your wife again are we Senator Briggs?"

Barbie peered around Death Pillow's back to see who was in the spotlight.

A man with greying hair and a much younger woman on his arm was trying hard to hide from the camera The Mouth held.

FOUR EX-WIVES AND A WEDDING

The latest celebrity gossip internet sensation had an uncanny knack for being wherever the action was. Unlike his predecessors and peers, The Mouth scooped stories no one else knew even existed.

First to press was a big deal in the news world and everyone knew it. He was cornering the market, and everyone wanted to be his friend lest he turn his detective wit on their private life.

At the party for a second and he'd already bagged his first victim. Moving forward into the crowd, The Mouth, a six foot four man built like a professional wrestler and sporting both bleached, spiked hair and sports sunglasses at night (though neither complemented his sleeveless, black tuxedo), came straight for Barbie.

Or so it felt to her.

Used to getting attention from men, not that she was exactly happy about it, Barbie could feel her heart begin to bang in her chest.

Hot on The Mouth's heels, was a second camera, this one held by a tall, attractive woman with jet black hair.

The Mouth talked to the camera in his hand, switching between it filming him and the crowd continuously. Coming closer, he held out a hand which Death Pillow slapped in greeting. The two men bro' hugged.

"Hey there folks at home. This is me hanging here with Death Pillow, America's number one rap star."

"You know it," agreed Death Pillow. "I'm smoking hot with my words and I don't even have to show it."

"Well who do we have here?" The Mouth noticed Barbie for the first time.

His question had been aimed at Death Pillow who fumbled for a name and struggled to recall it because he'd never bothered to ask.

"I'm Barbie," said Barbie, trying not to sound too starstruck.

"Hey, what are you doing here, Mouth?" a new voice entered the conversation. It belonged to Roy McElroy, a muscular action movie star known for his violent streak off the screen as much as for his acting. "You're not on the guest list, Mouth. Why don't you get out of here?"

Turning the camera on himself and making a mock frightened face, The Mouth swung his lens back to the actor.

"This, folks, is what happens when you abuse steroids. Your brain and your junk shrivel up until all you have are muscles and a waning career as a once famous actor."

"Why you ..." McElroy swung for the camera meaning to tear it from The Mouth's hands.

He missed when The Mouth ducked out of the way and put people between them. The result was McElroy swiping a brightly coloured cocktail from someone's hand. It shot three feet to splash down a lady's white cocktail dress and her outraged shriek got everyone's attention.

A Small Breakthrough

Lieutenant Commander Martin Baker returned before things could get ugly in Carol Oswald's suite. He came back through the door with Ensign Waddle escorting the young man they chased.

"Oh, Rickie, what happened to your head?" begged Carol.

Of the three women in the suite, I figured her for his 'meemaw'; there was a vague facial resemblance.

"He ran into a wall," Martin explained. "Next time, when we tell you to stop, stop."

I doubted there was going to be a next time. I said he had guilt in his eyes when I saw them and I knew why.

"Did he say anything?" I enquired, hoping he might have just confessed to make my life easy. A check of my watch had already told me the chance to have dinner with Alistair was gone. The guests would be sitting down to eat in half an hour.

"Asked for a lawyer," Martin reported, a wry smile teasing the corners of his mouth.

Studying the young man's face, I took out my camera and snapped a shot before anyone had time to protest. Not that I cared if they did.

"Hey, why are you taking his picture?" demanded Carol. "Why did you chase him?"

"Why are any of you still here?" Imelda fired in her thoughts. "We didn't have anything to do with Lexington's death. We all loathed the woman and so did everyone else. Ask around. You won't have to look far to find someone who wanted her dead."

Her words rang in my head. I noted them, but did not reply. Instead, I fired the picture across to Molly. Only once I sent it my brain caught up to remind me Molly was no longer with Betty. I wanted the bride-to-be to confirm the young man being held by Ensign Waddle was the same one who delivered the cake to her suite. However, Betty was at the rehearsal dinner and Molly would have taken the chance to return to her own cabin to freshen up and grab some food.

Undefeated, I turned on him.

"Your name, please?"

He said nothing.

"I can look it up on central registry if you like. It won't take more than a few minutes."

He stayed silent for another second before grumpily muttering, "Aegon Oswald."

"Your grandson?" I faced Carol for confirmation.

Just like her grandson, she chose to try not replying. Imelda glared at me, but her attitude only gave me fire.

"Aegon delivered the cake to Betty Ross's suite earlier. I sent his picture to the security officer I have guarding her. I can wait to have Miss Ross confirm what I already believe, or you can admit the truth now."

None of the ladies, nor Aegon himself showed any sign they might provide a response. Aegon's eyes were locked firmly on the deck. The ex-wives, however, their eyes burned with righteous justice.

"Very well." I dismissed the ex-wives with my eyes, turning to look at Martin instead. "Lieutenant Commander Baker, please summon additional security. I would like all three of these ladies taken to separate interview rooms and held there." Their protests were as instant as they were predictable. Lives filled with privilege and having people do whatever they wanted had eroded their sense of vulnerability. I was challenging them, and it came as a shock that I had the power and authority to do so. "Aegon Oswald too, please."

"Okay, I did it," snapped Aegon, his eyes up to meet mine now. The anger at being caught was there, but it wasn't aimed at me. Aegon was glaring at his grandmother. "I delivered the cake, but it wasn't my idea."

Imelda shouted, "Don't say anything!"

I couldn't stop the chuckle escaping my lips. "It might be a little late for that." I didn't bother to say anything else to the ladies. They believed that if they continued to deny their involvement, I might somehow get bored and go away. "Now, if you please, Lieutenant Commander."

Imelda spat an insult in my direction and fell back into a huddle with her co-conspirators.

I would interview them all, one at a time, in private, and determined though they seemed to be, one of them would crack. Bit by bit I would uncover the truth. They were here to interrupt the wedding and ultimately to stop it from happening. That much I was sure about. Now I wanted to know why.

The wedding and their decision to mess with it was a backdrop – an insignificant feeder – to the real crime: the murder of Lexington Brand. The ex-wives were up to no good, but did that make them killers?

With the sound of approaching boots echoing along the passageway outside, I resigned myself to what was probably going to prove to be a long evening. There would be no champagne and cocktails for me, but one way or the other, I was going to uncover what was going on.

A Change in Atmosphere

By the time Felicity arrived outside on the crowded sun terrace, members of the ship's security team had already stepped in to calm the heated situation and escort The Mouth and his partner from the party. Lieutenant Commander Singh, the officer in charge of the small detachment assigned to watch over proceedings, was disappointed to find it was not the relaxed evening she'd expected.

First there came a report about a missing handbag. A Gucci clutch the girlfriend of a film star carelessly placed on a table wasn't there when she went to pick it up. There was nothing in it save for her phone, she claimed, but she wanted that back too.

The film star reacted to his girlfriend's tears with anger and accusations aimed at the security team who, in his opinion, were failing to do their jobs.

Before Singh could deal with that mess, a United States Governor reported that his Patek Philippe watch was missing from his wrist.

It was while listening to the governor and trying to avoid his wildly gesticulating arms that Lieutenant Commander Singh heard the commotion caused by The Mouth's gate crashing. This, at least, was something she knew how to deal with.

His mouth running the whole time, for that was his reputation, The Mouth resisted very little on his way to the exit. His girlfriend went too, but continued to film the whole time.

For Samira Singh, a twelve year veteran with a glowing career path ahead, the danger of being filmed doing or saying the wrong thing filled her head with dread.

It was largely for that reason that she failed to do anything when The Mouth paused in the doorway to shout one last thing.

"Hey, John!" he bellowed, his voice loud enough to be heard above the crowd. It hushed the chatter, many of the dinner guests tuning their ears to hear what the loudmouthed gossip monger might have to say to the groom. "Convenient that Lexie died, huh? Did you pay someone to do it, or get your hands dirty yourself?"

From the shocked gasps and instant ripple of comments and questions that followed, it was clear Lexington's death wasn't public knowledge. Lieutenant Commander Singh didn't even know who *Lexie* was, but understanding she should have removed the unwanted guests already, ushered him through the exit.

Felicity's feet ground to a stop just a yard onto the sun terrace. Heading for the future bride and groom to apologise for the intrusion to their private event, she heard The Mouth's shout and saw how John reacted.

The ageing billionaire, his cute, twenty-two-year-old fiancée on his arm, looked like he'd been hit with a freeze ray. Or was having a stroke. The people around him ... scrap that, everyone was either looking his way or turning around so they could.

On the spot, he mumbled something to Betty and tried to find a direction he could look where he didn't meet a set of questioning eyes.

Giving up, he acted like the powerful leader he was.

"Yes, everyone, my first wife, the famous actress Lexington Brand, was murdered earlier today. I can assure you all I had nothing whatsoever to do with it. While it is no secret that we loathed each other, if I were to arrange to kill someone, it wouldn't be one of my ex-wives." His voice carried over the silent crowd, their conversations paused to listen. With all eyes on the groom, Felicity was shocked when he then cracked a smile. "It would be one of my competitors, like Elon here," John laughed at his own joke, reaching out to shake the hand of the man he'd just targeted.

Nervous titters went through the assembled guests.

Silence pervaded.

It was ten minutes early, but to rescue the groom and the situation, Felicity spun around to jerk an arm at the steward standing next to the enormous dinner gong. In the dimly lit banquet hall, he had to squint to see the wedding planner's urgent arm movements but got the message.

A resounding 'Dong!' rang out, pulling eyes and faces around to the awning erected to funnel guests inside the banquet room.

"Ladies and Gentlemen," Felicity announced, though it was supposed to be the master of ceremonies doing it, "dinner is served."

Commander Mophuthing skidded to a stop by her side, taking over with a confident smile.

Stepping to one side, Felicity jumped half out of her skin when Mindy appeared.

"What was that all about, Auntie?"

"Which bit?"

Mindy's eyebrows waggled in wonder. "I heard a scream," she said. "Well, everyone heard it. I was in the kitchen like you told me to be," Mindy omitted the part about chatting to the cute sous chef with the dimples, "making sure everything was on track," she hadn't been paying the slightest attention to what was happening, "and it sounded like someone had been stabbed."

"That was just a cocktail going down someone's dress." It pained Felicity that she hadn't been able to get to the lady. The Mouth's shouts diverted her attention and by the time she looked again, the woman, a politician's wife, was gone.

Fixing her up with a new dress and getting her back to the party looking better than before was the sort of thing that made Felicity one of the top wedding planners. That process of being prepared for disasters and downscaling them swiftly into minor incidents was what got her the big clients.

Too late now, the lady in question was undoubtedly attending to the matter herself.

The cocktail to the dress was no big deal though, not when compared to the repercussions of The Mouth's revelation. On the eve (okay so technically it was the eve of the eve) of the groom's wedding, the guests learned his first wife had been murdered.

Stepping back inside the banquet hall, Felicity could sense ... almost hear the change in atmosphere. It was all wrong. The happy mood that ought to dominate was missing. In its place suspicion, mistrust, and whispered conjecture filled the air.

The guests were taking their seats, a seating plan around the circular table structured so no one could complain they were positioned at the end as they would had there been a long table or a horseshoe arrangement.

Betty and John, minus John's eldest son, Tim, whose mother had been murdered a few short hours ago and was understandably absent, waited to one side with Betty's immediate family. Felicity sucked in a deep breath through her nose.

The Ross family were not her usual clientele. It was not her nature to judge, but there was no way to avoid how out of place they were among the rich, the famous, and the powerful. That they were supporting Betty because they hoped to cash in was something they didn't even bother to hide.

They were appropriately dressed at least. Well mostly. Betty's closest sibling, a seventeen-year-old boy called Skidz (his real name), was wearing a black dinner jacket, but the bow tie was already hanging loose where he'd chosen to undo it, and his outfit was augmented by Converse high top sneakers and a West Ham United ball cap.

Felicity told herself it was the best she could hope for. Provided they behaved, she didn't care what they wore.

At a nod of her head, the master of ceremonies announced the wedding party and led them to their seats. Polite applause welcomed Betty and John.

"You seem worried, Auntie," observed Mindy.

"That's because I am. Can you not feel the tension in the room?"

Mindy shrugged. "It always feels like this, Auntie. You worry too much; it's going to be fine."

It wasn't though. Wait staff descended on the circular table, positioning themselves behind the guests and waiting until they were all in place before they stepped forward as one to start dispensing wine to accompany the first course.

Felicity was daring to relax when the first cries of alarm rang out.

Looking through the same window which Mindy had earlier used to spy on Carol, the man in the scruffy suit nodded his head and turned away.

Too Tired

"Patricia dear, you work too hard," Lady Mary scolded me. "Far too much rushing around if you ask me."

I hadn't and I could easily have reminded her how I came to her rescue when a band of treacherous handlers at her zoo attempted to murder her and everyone else so they could auction off her animals and vanish with the money. She had not thought my rushing around was a bad thing then. Of course, I chose to agree with her because she was not only right – I do work too hard – but also because she was only trying to be my friend.

The ex-wives were in their separate interview rooms, each left to stew by themselves for I was in no rush. The tactic of making them wait was an old one. Leave them long enough and they would be begging to tell all when I finally showed my face.

Or maybe they wouldn't. These were not your average petty criminals and though I was yet to determine what was at stake, I had a feeling the stakes were higher than usual. If it was John's fortune on the line, then we were talking about billions of dollars. There was something else of course – the thing Lexington knew and John refused to disclose.

That bothered me.

A secret so powerful a man would cancel his wedding to avoid it being revealed. I saw his eyes when Lexie threatened to say it in my presence. The panic and fear he felt were real.

Retreating to my suite provided the opportunity to check on my dogs. Jermaine assured me Anna and Georgie had drained their water bowl and were asleep on the couch within a minute of arriving. For them the day was done and they had no reason to be awake until bedtime biscuits arrived.

Time to think was another reason to delay the interviews, but with Lady Mary in my suite it was no shock that I had a gin and tonic in my hand.

I wasn't complaining. In fact, the delicious drink made me question the merits of sending a few down to the ex-wives. Perhaps a little gin would loosen their tongues.

I hadn't eaten my risotto before I went out and Jermaine assured me it was no good for reheating now. He offered to fix me umpteen different dishes, all of which could be prepared in short order, but disappointing him and apologising while doing so, I asked him to arrange some sushi to be delivered.

Lady Mary approved.

"I haven't had really good sushi since I was last on board," she remarked. "I went to a Japanese place in Covent Garden not so very long ago; people were raving about how fresh and succulent it was. I just thought it was overpriced. I mean it wasn't bad," she said, selecting a California roll from our selection platter, "but one doesn't take the helicopter all the way to London for 'not bad'."

With five hundred guests attending the wedding, Lady Mary was one of the four hundred not attending the wedding breakfast. No doubt some saw it as a snub; I knew that happened at standard, everyday weddings just from talking to my friends. Was it worse at big celebrity bashes where amplified self-importance would make people believe they were too famous or rich to be left out?

Probably.

Lady Mary did not seem to care.

Jermaine let me know that Barbie had gone celebrity spotting at the rehearsal dinner and managed to get herself invited inside by a rap star without a date for the night. I couldn't say I approved of my young friend accompanying another man to a formal event, but things had changed since I was in my twenties.

"What will happen if you leave your interviews until the morning and have a few more drinks with me, sweetie?" asked Lady Mary while upending her glass.

I snorted a laugh. "I would imagine Purple Star would hear about it, arrange a formal inquiry into the case, and fire me on the spot."

"Sounds like a solid plan then," she remarked, holding her glass aloft for Jermaine to refill.

I finished my drink too, but rather than ask for another, I set it back on the coffee table.

"Sorry, Mary, I doubt I will be back before bedtime and when I do return, I expect to want nothing more than to climb into bed."

"Your loss, sweetie," she replied, nodding her head gratefully at Jermaine upon accepting a fresh glass.

Perhaps it was, but the drive to solve Lexington's murder and acquire a written confession for the cake of threat plus a plausible reason for their plan was enough to get me out of my nice, comfortable suite again.

When I returned three hours later, the only light illuminating my rooms came from a table lamp close to my bedroom door. Felicity and Mindy would be staying at the rehearsal dinner until well after midnight, I imagined, supervising the event to make sure it all went to plan. I was guessing though; they could be in their beds already for all I knew. Barbie would be tucked up in bed, either here or in Hideki's cabin unless she was still having fun at the party I knew would follow the dinner, Lady Mary would have passed out from all the gin, and Jermaine – bless him – had taken himself through to his adjoining cabin.

He used to stay up until my return. Thankfully, after several stern lectures, he no longer did.

I found the dachshunds in my bedroom, the pair of girls sniffing below the door to check it was me and running up my legs when I tried to get in.

"Yes, yes, girls, mummy is here. I really haven't been gone all that long."

With the dogs trotting along in my wake, I took out my earrings and unclipped the strap on my watch. Settling on my dressing table stool, I stared into the mirror.

The ex-wives were proving tougher to crack than expected. Carol admitted to sending the cake with the vile message hidden between the layers – how could she do anything else after her grandson blurted his confession? However, they continued to provide alibis for each other. When they left John's suite, they went to a bar. There they remained until just after six o'clock when they moved to Carol's suite.

The timeline matched the search of their rooms, and the bar staff on shift at the time were able to confirm they saw all three ladies in the bar. Here's the thing though: bars on board are busy. This applies doubly when the ship is just setting sail. Any bar with a view of the harbour fills as passengers gather to watch wherever we are leaving vanish slowly into the distance.

What I mean is this: the ex-wives probably were all there, but the bar staff were too busy to know if one or more of them left and came back. From the bar they were inside - on the top deck - it was a ten-minute walk to the bank of elevators where Lexington was killed.

Carol's firecrackers, which she continued to deny any knowledge of, were enough for me to justify confining her to her suite. With a guard placed outside, I could be sure Carol would cause no further mischief.

I did the same to the other two. Fiona accepted her sentence meekly. Imelda the firebrand spewed a torrent of abuse and threats though the result was no different. Confining paying passengers to their cabins is shaky ground, but suspected of conspiring to murder Lexington and known to be responsible for sabotaging the wedding was all the justification I needed.

That wasn't enough though. It only dealt with the ex-wives' desire to mess with John and Betty's ceremony. If they were guilty of Lexie's murder, I still needed to find evidence and figure out why. Beyond the simple fact they all hated her, I mean.

FOUR EX-WIVES AND A WEDDING

The bloodwork from John's shirt still wasn't back; another open avenue I wanted to close. While quizzing Imelda, a vague theory formed in my head. If she killed Lexington – I could see her more willing to stab a person in the back than the other two – then it would be easy for her to get close to John and leave blood on his shirt.

I needed to ask John if that could be the case or not. Had he seen Imelda or Carol or even Fiona after he kicked them out of his suite? However, when Lieutenant Commander Baker escorted me to John's suite on the way back from the interviews, we got the Butler, Bartholomew instead.

"Mr Oswald has retired for the night, Mrs Fisher."

The response surprised me. I was half expecting him to still be having drinks after the party, and I came to his suite to see if some of the men might have retired there rather than compete with the always-too-loud music in the bar. That he was already in bed sounded wrong and I probably should have questioned it there and then.

Should I wake him? I debated the question in my head for a few seconds before deciding it wasn't necessary.

Martin asked, "There is no guard here?"

Bartholomew shook his head. "No, sir. Lieutenant Bhukari did not return with Mr Oswald."

Speaking to me, Martin said, "I'll stay here until I can arrange a guard to replace me." We knew Deepa had stayed with John until it was time to attend the dinner and accompanied him to it. There she left him, liaising with her husband and joining the interview efforts. Someone was supposed to bring him back to the suite, but the duty fell down somewhere.

Stifling a yawn, I decided at the time that quizzing John could wait until dawn. Lying in bed now, I wondered if that had been a wise choice. I favoured the exes over the groom, but forcing myself to keep an open mind, I knew I ought to have pushed through my fatigue and found out if one of them could have placed the blood on his cuff.

The argument still raged inside my head when sleep took me a few minutes later.

Glasses and Silverware

"Come on, Patty!" Barbie jogged on the spot at the foot of my bed. "It's a beautiful day outside and my ankle is finally feeling strong enough to go for a jog around the deck."

"Oh, hurrah," I replied sarcastically, my head barely lifted off the pillow. Barbie twisted her left ankle a while back when we were running away from criminals across rough countryside. I was glad to hear it was feeling better, but couldn't see why her improved health meant I had to suffer.

"Shall I shackle the sausages?" she asked, stretching in place to show how bendy she was. "Would you like to go for a run too, Georgie? Would you? Would you, sweet girl? I'll bet you would. Yes, shall Auntie Barbie take you for a nice run?"

The dachshunds answered by digging their way deeper under the covers.

Accepting that the sleep portion of my night was over, I levered my head away from the fine Egyptian cotton pillowcase encasing the wonderfully light yet stuffed goose down pillow, rolled over, and grumpily swung my legs out of the bed.

"I need ten minutes to wake myself up."

"You've got five, Patty. Not a moment longer or we'll do some interval exercises between laps." She jogged out of my bedroom.

I glanced back at my pillow and wondered what she would do if I went back to sleep. She would ditch a jug of water over my head, that's what she would do. You might now be questioning why I don't just kick her out and tell her what to do with her early morning runs, but the unpleasant truth is that she is operating on my instructions.

I did this to myself.

Way back when I first came on the ship I had low self-esteem – I'd just caught my husband with another woman – and body image issues that drove me to want to lose weight. Long story short, I met Barbie, and she helped me shed some unwanted pounds. Did I need to lose them? No, not really, but I did, and I will admit that the days when I subjected myself to strenuous exercise were those that I felt the most positive about the world.

Anyway, I forced her to swear that she would continue to beat me into exercising and to refuse to listen to my whining and excuses.

And that was why I was getting out of bed at five to six on a morning when I could legitimately claim I had good reason to stay in bed.

Twenty minutes later, Barbie made me glad I had.

"Say that again!" I demanded, managing to blurt the words between wheezing gasps of air.

"The rehearsal dinner never happened. How do you not know that? Didn't Felicity tell you?"

I showed her my face and the raised eyebrow it sported.

"I guess not then. Well, it was going badly because The Mouth gate crashed and started causing trouble … you know John's ex-wife was murdered, right?"

I'd barely seen Barbie yesterday and with no time to exchange stories, had failed to enlighten her on my latest investigation.

"That's what kept me from attending the dinner last night," I panted, losing yet more oxygen from my lungs.

"Right. So, anyway The Mouth was doing what he does, stirring things up and filming the celebrities behaving badly, but on his way out he shouted at the groom to ask if he paid someone to kill his ex-wife or did it himself."

My mouth might have dropped open if I wasn't already struggling for breath. I stopped running, needing to get some more air in if I was going to talk.

Barbie slowed and came back but didn't stop running. While she jogged in place, I was trying to work enough oxygen into my body to be able to ask a question.

"You're going to ask what happened next?" she guessed.

I gave her a thumbs up.

"Samira Singh escorted The Mouth out before Mr Oswald could say anything, but the damage was done. Lexington's death was big news so everyone around me started whispering and guessing. It was really uncomfortable going into dinner. Felicity called everyone in early. I think she was trying to move the event along from the awkwardness The Mouth's question caused."

"Did that work?" I asked, finally feeling like I could speak without keeling over.

"Not even slightly. Well, to be fair it might have. The people around me ... I tried to get a seat next to Liam Hemsworth, but Samuel L Jackson got in the way."

"Wait, is he the one who plays Thor?"

"No, that's his older brother Chris."

I'm not one for lusting after men I see on screen, but the chap playing Thor was one sexy hunk of meat.

Barbie shook her head to break her daydream. "Where was I?" She had a faraway look and her face aimed to the sky in thought. "Oh, yes," she found her way back to where she left off. "The people around me were still talking about whether it was true and Lexington had been murdered and how it was that the rehearsal dinner was going ahead with her body still cooling in the morgue. It was all a little unsettling. None of that mattered though because the stewards brought the wine and that's where dinner came to a sudden, yet rather explosive halt."

Confused about what that meant, I sought clarification.

"All the glasses leaked. Wine was going everywhere. They were serving beef carpaccio, so it was red wine, and the guests were diving to get away from the spreading mess before it went on their clothes."

"Leaked? How does a glass leak?"

"They had holes in them. Tiny little holes." Seeing me scrunch up my face, Barbie said, "Come on, I'll show you."

I'd just wrestled my heartrate back under control, but Barbie was already running again. With a grunt of effort, I forced my backside into gear, huffing and puffing along behind the perfect blonde athlete who was yet to break a sweat.

The banquet room had been reset from last night to be ready to seat the hundreds of passengers who would come for breakfast. The upper deck restaurant was one of the biggest and most popular places for food on the whole ship and it wasn't reserved for only those staying in the plushest suites. Its size and location dictated it would be repurposed whenever a special event demanded the space and views it provided.

I recalled an episode of Dancing with the Stars, the Indian version, being recorded there one fateful night. The banquet room looked so different on that occasion it was hard to imagine how the transformation was possible.

Barbie led me through the double doors and toward the kitchen at the back. Coming up on six thirty in the morning, a few early risers were in the restaurant already, but attendance was sparse. By eight o'clock the place would be packed with a queue outside.

Our passing drew no eyes until we got into the kitchen. I stopped to scoop my dogs. Pausing inside the door with eyes swinging our way. Chef Steinbeck spotted me, the skin either side of his eyes tightening when they narrowed.

On my second night aboard the Aurelia, which feels like a lifetime ago now, I posed as a chef to catch a killer. I was after the wrong man, but didn't figure that out until later. Chef Steinbeck was yet to forgive me for messing around with his perfectly oiled machine, but I was dating the captain and in theory, at least, I probably outranked him.

He eyed me with suspicion, but said nothing.

Near to us, a young woman in chef's garb said, "Hi, Barbie." She had a mixing bowl under one arm and a whisk in the other hand. "You looking for someone?"

"The glasses from last night. The ones with the holes in. Where did they go?"

"In the trash," replied Chef Steinbeck, his tone terse and impatient. "Where else would they go?" He was answering Barbie but looking at me, so he got my response.

"They are evidence, Chef Steinbeck. I need them."

A smirk crossed his face, there for a moment and banished before it could fully form.

"Terribly sorry," the German chef said, mimicking my English accent badly. "Nothing left but shards now."

Gritting my teeth, I went again. "Where? I need them."

I guess he sensed that I was going to persist. With a shrug, he turned his head slightly to one side, to shout, "Holland!"

"Yes, Chef?"

"Take Mrs Fisher to dig through the trash. Do not do it yourself. I want you back on the hollandaise in two minutes, understand?"

"Yes, Chef."

Happy to dismiss Chef Steinbeck and be out of his presence, I followed Holland across the kitchen. Was it the pressure of the job that drove the head man to be so abrupt and obnoxious all the time? Did it require that kind of toughness to succeed? He was the chef in the ship's top restaurant. If that wasn't a mark of ability, I couldn't imagine what was.

Barbie touched Holland's arm. "Why does he call you Holland?"

"Because I'm from Amsterdam. Chef says he has neither the time nor the inclination to learn our names. He says we are all so lacking in talent we probably won't last long enough under his stewardship for it to matter. He calls everyone by where they are from."

"What a great leader," I remarked. "So inspirational."

Holland, or whatever his name really was, twisted to shoot me a grin.

"He's really not that bad. I've learned a lot."

Barbie frowned. "But what if there are two people from the same place."

"Oh, he just makes up somewhere for them to be from. Canada is from Kenya, but we already had a Kenyan." Holland cut off any more questions, by pointing down a narrow passageway. "Here we are. Down here."

Holland led us to a series of hatches at chest height. Each had a label such as 'general waste', 'tins and glass', 'cardboard and paper'. They fed bins which would then be offloaded whenever we made port. For a horrifying moment, I worried the hatches might plummet through the ship to a waste area deep down in the ship. Sifting through the waste from the entire ship was not a task I relished. I needn't have worried though.

With a flourish, Holland opened a door below the hatch for glass and tin to reveal the broken glasses and empty tins it held.

"You'll want to be careful," he pulled a face as he peered inside. "There's a lot of smashed glass in there."

I took a look too, bending at the waist to place my face over the trash receptacle. What I should also have done was hold my breath. The food bin would have been worse, no doubt, but the mishmash of smells from whatever drinks the glasses once contained mixed with the food left in the tins gripped my stomach and threatened to empty it.

Ducking back, I snatched some cleanish air, held my breath and plucked a semi-intact wine glass from the top layer.

Barbie had retreated a yard, her nose wrinkling from the smell.

"HOLLAND!" roared Chef Steinbeck, his voice carrying from the kitchen.

"I'd better go," said Holland with a resigned sigh. "Anything else you need?"

I had the glass above my head, turning it in the light. Focussed on that, I almost ignored the young chef's question until Barbie spoke.

"Patty."

"What? Oh, yes, sorry. No, I think this is all I need."

I went back to holding the glass to the light. Barbie steered me from the kitchen - clearly what Holland was waiting for - my mind whirling.

The glass did indeed have little holes in it. One on either side, set not quite opposite each other as though the person making the holes was rushing to get it done or accuracy wasn't important.

"Have you seen these?" I asked.

We were back outside in the top deck restaurant where a few more passengers were coming through the main doors. The sun wasn't up yet but it would crest the horizon soon. Today was a sailing day, one where the people on board had to enjoy the facilities the ship offered. Tomorrow morning, our arrival in New York would be timed so people were awake to capture snaps as we sailed in past the Statue of Liberty.

It would be a standout moment for many passengers if they had never been to the famous city before.

Barbie said, "I saw it last night. I should have thought to grab one then, but I was caught up in the stampede of people all looking to get away. They were saying the wedding is doomed."

"They? Who's they?"

Barbie shrugged. "Just general 'they'. I heard a few people arguing about it as we left. John was imploring them to stay, and I think a few did, but the dinner was ruined by then. I don't know what the guests did instead, but I went to bed."

We were halfway to the doors to leave the restaurant, the scent of bacon and fresh coffee tugging at my hunger when I heard Chef Steinbeck again.

"Mrs Fisher?"

At least he was addressing me politely for once.

"Mrs Fisher, sorry, do you have a moment?"

I stopped and waited for him to come to me.

"What can I do for you?"

"I was going to report this later," he wheezed, a little out of breath from crossing the restaurant, "but since you are here…"

"What it is you need to report?"

"Theft, Mrs Fisher. We are missing about ten percent of our silverware from last night. It is counted out and counted back in. Ten complete dinner sets are missing plus cruet sets and a few other accompanying items."

"That's a lot of silver," I frowned. "Any idea what might have happened to it?"

Chef Steinbeck nodded vigorously. "Yes, actually. I have it on good authority the bride's family were seen in the area where we keep it."

I tried hard to keep my face passive; I didn't want to show the news came as no surprise.

"Thank you, Chef. I will be sure to look into it."

"It's a lot of silver," he reminded me. "Couldn't easily be carried by one person."

No, but a family could shift it easily.

"Please excuse us, we really must get on with our investigations." I gave Chef Steinbeck a curt nod and left him to return to his work. I was going to have to tackle the problem of the Ross family, but there were higher priority tasks that came first.

Outside the restaurant, I held the glass up to the light again.

"What do you suppose could make a hole like that? It's tiny."

Barbie didn't know which came as no surprise, and an internet search – she was on her phone a second after I posed the question – yielded no answers either.

Squinting at it, Barbie remarked, "You would think it would break. You couldn't use a regular drill."

I felt certain she was right and could offer no brilliant insight into how a person might have drilled one hole, let alone the dozens Barbie assured me had spewed wine across the dining tables last night.

Thoughts of tiny glass eating insects randomly filling my head were chased away by the ringing of my phone. With a fight, I wrestled it from the back pocket on my shorts, to find 'Dr Davis' displayed on the screen.

My heart leaping, I thumbed the green button and prayed for good news.

Lady Mary Turns Sleuth

Lady Mary woke to the sound of Patricia's dachshunds, Anna and Georgie, landing on her bed. Leaving her bedroom in the middle of the night to fetch a snack from the kitchen, she'd omitted to close the door upon her return.

Yawning and covering her mouth with the back of her free hand, she carried the plate to the kitchen with the dogs dancing by her feet. The plate had been on the nightstand next to her head, a location which guaranteed the dogs tried to go over her face to reach it.

Truly awake at least an hour earlier than her usual time to rise, she wanted coffee and found Jermaine was way ahead of her.

"Good morning, Lady Mary. May I offer you some breakfast?"

"Oh, goodness, no, dear. It's far too early to think about eating something. I'll stick with the coffee thanks, though a Bloody Mary or a mimosa wouldn't go amiss." Looking around, she asked, "Where is Patricia?"

"Mrs Fisher is out for her morning run with Miss Berkeley, Lady Mary."

Lady Mary shuddered.

Jermaine untied his pinafore, lifting it over his head to fold it neatly.

"Are you leaving, dear?" Lady Mary enquired, her coffee cup clutched between two grateful hands.

Jermaine folded the apron again and dropped it into a drawer on the far side of the freestanding breakfast bar.

"If you do not currently need me, Lady Mary, I shall take the dogs for a walk."

"Oh, I can do that, sweetie," Lady Mary volunteered, surprising herself. "I think some fresh air will do me good. Maybe Patricia will be back by the time I return."

Jermaine dipped his head. "As you wish, Lady Mary."

While Lady Mary changed her clothes and donned a pair of suitable shoes, Jermaine shackled the sausage dogs.

Taking their leads, Lady Mary set off for a walk to clear her head. It was her intention to head out onto the deck. Temperatures were dipping now they were sailing north, but it wasn't cold and the dogs would benefit from the sea air. However, less than a hundred yards later, and before she could get to the first set of doors to access the deck, she spotted the man with the ill-fitting suit. He'd changed his clothes, not that his latest outfit was much of an improvement, but it was definitely him.

He didn't see her, he was facing the other way to look down over the drop to the next deck, and curious about who he could be, Lady Mary settled in to watch.

The man was in his late fifties with hair going thin and starting to recede. His clothes didn't fit very well – they were all too big for him as though he'd recently lost a lot of weight or was wearing someone else's outfit.

He didn't exactly look dangerous. Devious maybe, Lady Mary decided. Tucked behind one of the ship's giant potted plants, she tried not to look like she was spying and had to duck the eyes of several passing passengers when their looks questioned what she was up to.

FOUR EX-WIVES AND A WEDDING

A minute later she was just starting to question if she was being ridiculous when the man set off. He'd spotted something on the next deck that had him instantly moving with purpose.

"Come along, Mary. It's time to show Patricia she's not the only sleuth in town."

The dachshunds pulled against their collars, their little feet scrambling on the marble deck in their haste to give chase. Lady Mary assumed they were simply keen to go somewhere and wouldn't find out until later the real reason why the dachshunds were in such a hurry to follow the scruffy man.

At the bottom of the escalator, Lady Mary stepped off, pausing to plop the sausage dogs back on the deck having carried them on the ride down. The man was fifty yards ahead and moving with the flow of passengers making their way toward the restaurants serving breakfast.

The dachshunds continued to strangle themselves in their bid to close the gap.

"Let's not get too close, ladies, eh? We don't want Mr Sneaky Trousers to spot us, now do we?"

Certain the man she tailed had seen someone on deck nineteen who he was now following, Lady Mary was doing her best to figure out who it might be. There were hundreds of people about and the scruffy man's target could be any one of those moving ahead of him.

It wasn't anyone though. The man's target showed himself a heartbeat later when he turned into a restaurant and stopped at the menu board. Lady Mary knew precisely who he was: Roger Oswald, John Oswald's youngest son. She hadn't seen him in years, not since he was a teenager, but there was no mistaking the scar on his neck, the result of brash youthfulness in his high school days. The prank had almost killed him the way she remembered hearing the tale.

The scruffy man didn't stop or follow Roger Oswald into the restaurant. In fact, he carried on by as though he wasn't following him at all. However, he glanced back, looking directly at Roger Oswald with a deep frown etched onto his face.

He didn't see her; his attention was all on Roger, but Lady Mary ducked behind a palm tree anyway. When she peered out a few seconds later, the scruffy man was nowhere to be seen.

She searched fruitlessly for five minutes, and returned to ask Roger if he knew why he was being followed. Roger wasn't there either. For whatever reason – perhaps the breakfast offerings didn't suit him. Roger Oswald was nowhere in sight.

Perplexed, but feeling exhilarated, Lady Mary had one last look around before accepting defeat. Hungry now that the breakfast smells had infiltrated her nostrils, she tugged at the dogs leads to get them moving back toward the escalators. She might have lost her quarry, but she had plenty to tell Patricia.

Watching as the elegant woman with Patricia Fisher's dachshunds – he would recognise the little dogs anywhere – rode the escalator back to the top deck, the scruffy man narrowed his eyes.

Body Count

"Mrs Fisher, good morning. You asked that I alert you when I got the lab results back from the blood on John Oswald's shirt."

I spasmed with excitement. "Dr Davis, good morning. Thank you for calling."

Barbie and I were on our way to Betty's suite on deck nineteen to see how she was. Chances were that her family would be there to give their support though I wasn't convinced the bride-to-be had that close of a relationship with them. Truthfully, I wanted to see how they would react when they saw me again and hoped they were there.

I wasn't going to level any accusations; not yet - dealing with their petty thefts would tie up my time when I needed to be focused on a murder, but I did want to gauge how guilty they looked.

Praying Dr Davis was about to say the blood on John's shirt had not come from Lexington Brand, I held my breath.

"It's Lexington Brand's blood all right."

"Rats!"

Barbie raised her eyebrows, wondering what might be getting me so excited.

Dr Davis's news was the last thing I wanted to hear and ran against everything I had allowed myself to believe. So far as evidence went, it was right up there next to smoking guns and fingerprints. I had been ready to bet there was someone else behind Lexington's death, but that seemed unlikely now.

"You are absolutely sure?" I fired back.

"It's a one hundred percent match, Patricia. There's no question the blood came from Lexington Brand. How it got there is not something I care to speculate on."

I thanked Dr Davis and let him go.

"Not the result you wanted?" asked Barbie. We were nearing Betty's suite, but armed with new information, I no longer wanted to go in. The blood analysis meant her intended was most likely guilty of murder and that wasn't something I could pretend to not know while making chitchat about a wedding that wouldn't happen.

I stopped walking so I could think. John's guilt still didn't feel right. My senses were pushing against the verdict like two similar magnetic poles being shoved toward each other – no matter how hard I tried, my brain refused to accept it.

"I need to talk to John." It was a simple announcement and made so swiftly that I left Barbie behind when I set off.

Whether I liked it or not, I was going to have to lock John up. Or confine him to his suite under armed guard – something that would guarantee the safety of the other passengers on board and show I was doing my job. My gut might yet prove itself right, but until I gathered the evidence to back up my beliefs, I couldn't justify letting him wander around free.

Rounding the next corner with Barbie by my side, I did my best to explain what she didn't know. For once my blonde friend hadn't been involved in the investigation, but before I was halfway done, we ran into Sam and Pippin. They were in the passageway ahead of us and coming our way at a jog.

"You heard already?" Lieutenant Pippin's creased brow showed his confusion.

FOUR EX-WIVES AND A WEDDING

"Heard what?"

Pippin's mouth formed an 'O'.

"Someone's dead," beamed Sam like it was great news, a smile never far from his face regardless of the situation.

Shock registered and my mind scrambled. Who was dead? My first thought was it might be Betty and the boys were heading in the right direction if they were going to her suite. Molly was with her though and Pippin would be moving a lot faster if his girlfriend was in trouble.

I didn't have to ask, of course, Pippin didn't make me wait.

"It's Fiona Sugarman. We got a tip off and sent Ensign Rostova to check inside her cabin. She was killed in the night, stabbed while she slept."

Another knifing. I felt a little sick.

Barbie had a question, "Hold on. Mrs Sugarman is one of John Oswald's ex-wives, right?"

"Yes."

"So, if Ensign Rostova was guarding the door to her suite, how did someone get inside and kill her?" Barbie made a valid point. "She's on this deck, yes?"

She was and we knew what that meant: her suite had no adjoining butler's cabin. I myself had utilised the butler's entrance to get in and out of my suite when the main door was being guarded.

Meeting the guys in the passageway, we had ground to a halt, the four us of still standing there when we needed to be heading to Fiona's suite.

Snapping out of it, we got moving. We were not the first to arrive though, Martin Baker and Schneider beat us to it.

Ensign Rostova was inside, sitting in a chair with his head down. How someone got in was fairly obvious: the guard had wandered off. It wasn't necessarily Rostova to blame, however. It wasn't like he would have been stationed on the door all night. Half a dozen or more of the security team's most junior members would have rotated through the duty of keeping Mrs Sugarman in her cabin. Only once we knew the time of death could we better pinpoint who might have failed in their duty.

First things first, I forced my feet to carry me through to the bedroom where Lieutenant Schneider was staring down at the body.

Mercifully, it wasn't a frenzied attack with blood splatter in every direction. In fact, one could be forgiven for thinking Fiona was still asleep. Her covers were around her chin and her limbs were all tucked in nice and warm.

The bloody hole in the sheets was the only indicator anything might be amiss. A single stab wound was what it looked like. The killer entered her bedroom and struck while she slept. Fiona never even got a chance to defend herself.

Whatever my opinion of the woman, she hadn't deserved to be murdered in her bed.

I walked back to the suite's main living area.

"Ensign Rostova?"

"Yes?" he lifted his head, his eyes and facial expression vacant from the shock of finding the woman dead.

"You lifted the sheets to check her condition?" I asked; it was important to establish what other genetic evidence there might be around her body. I suspected there to be only a slim chance the killer would have left their DNA behind.

"Yes, Mrs Fisher. Should I not have?"

"No, it's fine. You did the right thing."

Martin said, "I've got someone bringing me a roster of those who were on duty last night. I'll bet this month's wages one of them wandered away at some point."

"Or was lured," said Pippin, ominously.

FOUR EX-WIVES AND A WEDDING

"Or was lured," I repeated, the words bouncing around my skull. Two of John's ex-wives were dead, and I already knew his movements could not be accounted for after the rehearsal dinner was aborted. Having dropped John off at the banquet hall, Deepa Bhukari was with me. When the dinner subsequently ended hours before it should, John found himself free to roam.

Did that coincide with the time of death?

"Is the doctor aware?" I asked.

Pippin answered, "Dr Nakamura is on his way."

I had Martin confirm there was still a guard outside John's door and settled in to wait. Not for long, thankfully.

Dr Hideki Nakamura arrived moments later, his doctor's bag held in his left hand.

"Another one?" he asked grimly.

All I could do was nod.

Pippin led Hideki through to the bedroom where he confirmed death and started to examine Fiona's body.

"A single puncture wound," he remarked, leaning in close to get a good look. "From the angle I would guess it entered the left ventricle. Death would have been almost instantaneous. You say she is linked to the previous victim?"

"They were both married to John Oswald in the past. Fiona was his second wife. Lexington was his first."

Sam asked, "Who is number three?"

My eyes shot up to meet his, then whipped around to stare at Martin.

"Has anyone checked on the other ex-wives?" My question matched the thoughts in Martin's head who was already reaching for his radio.

My heart beat way too fast for the next minute until confirmation came back that Carol and Imelda were both still alive.

Trying to calm my frayed nerves, I asked, "Can you estimate time of death?"

I got the usual, "I'll need to perform a full autopsy," reply doctors always give, but Hideki was good enough to throw me a rough guess.

"Between ten and midnight last night given the state of rigor."

Ten and midnight. The rehearsal dinner went south just after eight. It was gone eleven when I got to John's suite to have Bartholomew tell me he was asleep which meant the ex-wives were returned to their cabins no earlier than ten-thirty. Either John pounced the moment Fiona returned or Bartholomew assumed his principal was asleep when really John wasn't even in the suite. Whatever the case, there were three hours of movement unaccounted for when John wasn't under guard. He's probably innocent, I told myself for the umpteenth time, but the voice in my head sounded less and less convinced all the time.

I had work to do, and it was going to start with finding out what John did when the party went south.

Unavoidable Evidence

If John was faking his shock at the news of Fiona's murder, he deserved an Oscar for his performance.

"I can't believe this is happening. Chris and Isabel will be devastated. Those are our children," he explained. "Then there are the grandchildren. Oh, this is terrible."

The billionaire sat slumped in an armchair next to a bookshelf in his suite. From the bags under his eyes I could tell he got too little sleep the previous night. The question, of course, was why? Was it just the drama of the rehearsal dinner playing on loop in his head? Or had he murdered two women in twenty-four hours?

"John, what time did you leave the rehearsal dinner last night?"

"What's that got to ... Now hold on, Patricia. You can't possibly think I had anything to do with Fiona's murder. What motivation could I possibly have?"

"The blood on your shirt was Lexington's, John," I levelled an accusation. "Do you expect me to believe you have no idea how it got there?"

His face took on a look of shock, but only momentarily. Then the attitude that made him a leader of industry kicked in.

"Yes, I damned well do, Mrs Fisher. I didn't kill Lexington and I certainly didn't kill Fiona. I loved that woman."

"Then why divorce her?"

"She left me," John revealed. Knowing he had to give me more, he explained, "She caught me cheating. With Carol." His final words were whispered, a shameful admission he would much rather no one knew.

For a moment I wondered if this gave Carol cause to want Fiona dead, but the two of them had been working together – to me an indication any bad blood had been laid to rest.

"What did Lexington hold over you?" I returned to a question he'd refused to answer every time I raised it.

"It is of no consequence!" John shouted, spittle flying from his lips as his face went red. "I will not discuss the subject. The matter died with her and while that may seem awfully convenient, I can assure you any time you spend investigating *me* will be a gift to the killer."

His bullish attitude wasn't helping. He was angry, but so was I. Two people were dead and if I wanted to find a person who stood to gain from both murders, it was John Oswald. Lexington had a hold over her ex-husband that allowed her to make him dance to her tune. And Fiona was part of a plot to disrupt John's wedding. Maybe there was another reason for him to want her dead, but it felt like I already had enough.

Like they say: the first murder is the hard one. After that they get easier and easier.

"John, I have no choice but to place you under arrest. Lieutenant Commander Baker will escort you to the brig where you will remain until I have some answers."

John swore and cursed, expressing his disappointment in me. He expected better; that was the crux of it. I was supposed to be able to figure out who was behind the murders, not accuse an innocent man.

FOUR EX-WIVES AND A WEDDING

There would be more questions later, and I wanted to find some more hard proof. The blood on his shirt, the secret he wouldn't share, and his inability or refusal to account for the times around the two deaths left me with no choice but to assume he was guilty.

I couldn't ignore the evidence in front of me however much I didn't want to believe it. It was enough to obtain a conviction I felt sure, though John would have some powerful lawyers to fight in his corner when it came to court.

John was led away by a pair of security officers, Martin leading them to make sure it was all done properly and to ensure a member of my team was at the helm. Schneider stayed behind with me to supervise the search of John's suite.

"Am I free to go?" asked Bartholomew, the butler, standing rigidly next to the kitchen counter.

I said, "Yes. I need you out, actually. I will have questions for you later though so please don't go far or make sure one of my officers has your phone number."

"Very good, Mrs Fisher." He gave a curt nod before retreating through the door to his adjoining cabin.

What I needed to do was return to my suite and get dressed for the day. I did not consider sportswear to be appropriate and would have changed already had yet another murder not denied me the chance.

However, before I could announce my intention to Lieutenant Schneider, my phone rang with a worrying call.

Murder Weapon

Lady Mary's call confused me, but hearing she was in my suite with Felicity, I chose to end the phone conversation and continue it in person. Barbie was also in my suite having split from me when I went to see Fiona. She'd been good enough to bring the others up to speed about the second murder.

We were not talking about that though. We were discussing the man Lady Mary followed.

"A scruffy man in a jacket?" My face was scrunched with the effort of trying to picture what Lady Mary was telling me.

She took a sip of gin and frowned at me. "He was there yesterday, Patricia. I cannot believe you don't know who I'm talking about."

"There where?"

"At the first murder scene," Lady Mary sounded as though she believed we had been through all this already, but it was news to me. "I said something to you at the time. Don't you remember?"

My shoulders hunched in a deep, apologetic shrug. "Maaaaybeeee," I drawled, wondering if Lady Mary's gin-addled, patchy memory was playing tricks on her and not wanting to voice my thoughts.

"Oh, for goodness sake. Nevermind. The point is he was there yesterday where Lexington was found and I'm sure I saw him again after that. Then, this morning he was just around the corner from here. From your suite, Patricia. I don't mean to be judgy, but he doesn't look like he can afford a suite on the top deck."

"Plenty of people come by here on their way to somewhere else. The top deck restaurant is open to all," I pointed out. "He could have just been exploring the ship."

Lady Mary's eyes sparkled. "A-ha! I thought you might say that. So answer me this, super sleuth. What was he doing following Roger Oswald?"

"Who is Roger Oswald?"

Felicity recited, "First son of Carol Oswald. John Oswald's third son. Divorced from his wife but has a son himself, called Aegon. Both Roger and Aegon were on the guest list," she explained how she knew so much.

Aegon, the man who delivered Carol's 'cake of threat', had his father on board and he had a mystery man following him. What was all that about?

I put a hand to my forehead and closed my eyes; the bombardment of information from three overlapping cases was already making it swim. Now I had Lady Mary's mystery man to squeeze in too.

"Did you see him do anything to Roger Oswald?"

"No," Lady Mary confirmed without needing to think. "No, he was just following him. Roger went into a restaurant on deck nineteen – one of the breakfast places – and the scruffy man carried on. He made it look natural, but he looked back, you see? Once he was a few yards past the restaurant, he turned his head and looked right at Roger Oswald. Whoever he is, he's up to no good. Maybe he's your killer and there are other people being targeted."

The new player was one I did not need. Everything about him sounded like a cliché and I wanted to dismiss him as a red herring.

I couldn't though. My skull had just itched.

A knock at my door made the dogs bark. They had fussed around my feet when I first came in, but they had breakfast in their bellies and Lady Mary had taken them for a walk – they were done for the morning and were on the couch until someone dared to beg entry.

They shot across the carpet to bark at the door or, rather, the person beyond it until Jermaine caught up to them and let our guest in.

Alistair was a sight for sore eyes, and I went to him.

He greeted me with a light kiss.

"You arrested John Oswald?" The captain missed very little, so he wasn't asking a question, merely starting a topic of conversation.

"I did. The evidence stacks against him."

Hearing the timbre of my voice, Alistair was quick to conclude, "But you don't think he did it?"

I puffed out my cheeks and shrugged. "I can't tell yet."

"Well," Alistair claimed a seat at the breakfast bar and gratefully accepted a cup of coffee from Jermaine, "I'm afraid I am not here with good news."

Inside I groaned. On the outside, I said, "Let's hear it."

"There were a number of thefts at the rehearsal dinner last night."

"I know. I spoke with Chef Steinbeck about his missing silver already. It's not going to make it to the top of the priority list any time soon."

Alistair's face made it look like the silverware was new information.

"I had not heard that report. I was referring, I'm afraid, to a number of the celebrities attending the dinner who discovered their wallets, purses, handbags and other such highly desirable designer brand items were missing. Much concern was raised about photographs a person might access by taking a celebrity's phone. There have been no ransom demands yet, but that is what is expected."

I could sense there was more.

When I said nothing, Alistair gave a sigh and revealed the final piece of detail.

"More than one person pointed their fingers at the Ross family."

Lady Mary snorted. "Hardly surprising, Alistair. Or did Patricia not tell you about her little run in with them yesterday?"

I had not and now I needed to. Alistair listened to the shoplifting story and how I handled it, giving no indication whether he approved or not. All the while, I thought about the Ross family and questioned what could possibly motivate them to pursue petty theft when Betty was about to marry a billionaire.

I was going to have to take officers to search their cabin, but I wasn't wrong that it would have to wait. Murder trumps theft every day of the week.

"Tell him about the scruffy man," insisted Lady Mary.

Alistair raised an eyebrow and for the next few minutes I went over the details of the case. I left Lady Mary to tell Alistair about the scruffy man while I took a fast shower and found clothes for the day.

Sitting on my bed a few minutes later, I looked outside where the sky was now a dull grey. The late autumn soon to give way to winter was bringing cold air and rainy weather the further north we went. It was such a contrast to Miami and the Caribbean before that. I selected a pair of trousers in a light grey colour and black ankle boots. On top a chunky knitted top in a jet black. I liked how I looked and prayed I wouldn't have to do any running.

In the kitchen, Jermaine was preparing me a breakfast of smoked salmon and scrambled eggs with chives and garlic. Together with two pieces of wholemeal toast it would provide the energy I needed to get through the day.

Barbie was at the breakfast bar eating what appeared to be kitty litter, but she assured me it was a nutritious food supplement filled with vitamins, minerals and the right amount of protein. Just so long as she didn't want me to eat it.

Alistair drank coffee next to Lady Mary.

"Where's Felicity?" I asked.

Barbie said, "Gone with Mindy to stand down all the wedding suppliers and to see the bride and her family."

That the wedding was off could not be doubted this time.

My phone rang, the screen showing Schneider's name.

"Schneider?"

"Mrs Fisher, we believe we have found the murder weapon. Are you free to return to the Platinum Suite?"

Jermaine was just serving my food and my stomach gave a desperate growl at the thought of being filled.

"I'll be ten minutes?" I offered.

"We'll keep looking for more evidence until you return."

I placed the phone to one side, thanked Jermaine, and tucked in. It was just what I needed. Hearing that the murder weapon was in John's suite was precisely the opposite of what I needed.

"The case against John Oswald is tight?" Alistair asked. He was making conversation, but also doing his job. He needed to be sure I was getting it right and savvy enough to know John's lawyers would come gunning.

I swallowed a forkful and dabbed my mouth with a napkin before responding.

"Yes and no." With everyone listening, I did my best to explain. "John is hiding something from his past." I explained about Lexington. "And he has no alibi for the times when the murders took place. Now it would seem the murder weapon has been found in his cabin and the first victim's blood is on his shirt. Right now the security officers in the brig will be confiscating his clothes so they can be analysed for Fiona's DNA. I don't know what we will find, but I believe it would be easy to convict."

"What do you think he might be hiding?" Alistair went straight for the key question.

Obviously, I had no answer, but said, "Something explosive."

"You want me to see if I can find anything?" Barbie volunteered.

Automatically, I opened my mouth to say she should not bother, but I changed my mind before the words reached the air. Barbie is a whizz on the internet. Her ability to find information startles me every time.

So instead of telling her not to, I said, "If you think you have time, sweetie."

Barbie pushed her bowl aside and rolled her shoulders like she was warming up for a fight.

"Yeah, it'll be fun. Jermaine will help me, won't you, babes."

"If madam has nothing else for me ..."

I smiled. "Of course not." Finishing the last bites of my breakfast. I too set my plate aside. In the last ten seconds a new determination had gripped me. John was innocent or guilty. One or the other. I had a day to figure it out.

Alistair came with me when I left, walking by my side, my arm looped through his. I left the dachshunds to snooze the morning away on the couch. They would be happier there and it was impractical to have them with me for interviews and crime scenes.

Diverting my attention, probably a deliberate tactic to make me think about something else, Alistair asked me about New York.

"I was there a couple of months ago, but I didn't really get to see anything." The ship didn't stop in the most famous of all American cities more than a couple of times a year, but that still meant Alistair had been there dozens of times in the course of his career. He liked to take me places, and there was no resistance from me. He knew all the best locations to visit, and we got to spend time together just the two of us, something that was next to impossible on board the ship.

My previous visit to New York happened when Barbie's little brother got himself into trouble. It was a case of wrong place wrong time for him, but we managed to sort things out with the help of some unexpected friends.

Strolling arm in arm around the ship to return to John's suite, we outlined a rough agenda and a list of places we could visit.

At the open door to the Platinum Suite the security officer on the door, another young ensign, snapped to attention at the sight of his captain. I stood on my tiptoes to kiss Alistair and send him on his way.

He needed to go be a captain and make the passengers feel special and I had more than one mystery to solve.

I guess the message that I was outside reached Lieutenant Schneider's ears because he arrived in the passageway keen to speak with me.

He interrupted my kiss.

"Oh, um, excuse me," he turned away, embarrassed. "Good morning, sir," he saluted Alistair.

I chuckled and pushed my beau away.

"Go on." I thought about smacking Alistair's bottom and stopped myself because there were crew watching. "Go do some work."

Alistair took a moment to speak with the young ensign guarding the suite's entrance when I went inside; he was always imparting wisdom and advice to his crew.

FOUR EX-WIVES AND A WEDDING

Inside the Platinum Suite I wasted no time, heading straight for the most damning piece of evidence: the murder weapon.

That's where things changed.

Framed

In the little cupboard under the sink in the bathroom attached to the Platinum Suite's master bedroom was a kitchen knife wrapped in a bloody towel. It was already in an evidence bag by the time I saw it, but there were photographs to show how it was found.

As a piece of evidence to secure a conviction it was right up there with a suspect saying, 'I'm glad I killed her.' Ordinarily, I would be rejoicing that it was all so clean and clear cut. Not today though.

Why?

Because it had been planted.

It must have been.

Lexington's blood on John's cuff was hard to explain away, this was harder still and that was the point. I held no doubt it would prove to be the blade that was used to kill both Lexington and Fiona; two women John Oswald had reason to want out of the way.

"Did you dust for prints?"

Schneider said, "Wiped clean."

Of course there were no prints. John was no fool, but I doubted he had ever touched it. Only a complete idiot would keep the murder weapon and tuck it away where it was bound to be found complete with the blood of the victim or victims. No, the real killer had put it here to ensure a court had all the evidence it could want. In so doing they had overstepped.

It was too much.

"Anything else?" I asked.

Schneider shook his head. "Not so far."

"No blood anywhere? No notes where John lays out his intricate plot to kill all his ex-wives?"

Schneider gave me a questioning look.

"Um, no, nothing like that."

I wiggled my lips around and puffed out my cheeks as I thought. "I need to speak with Tim Oswald."

John's eldest son and the heir to his empire was travelling with his father. They started out all staying in the same suite, but when his elderly father took up a relationship with the bubbly blonde English woman, Tim elected to move to a different suite. I guess he could afford to do that.

No sooner did I announce my desire to speak with him than he arrived. News of his father's arrest had reached Tim's ears and he was, shall we say, less than happy.

"Is she in there?" Tim demanded to know, his voice too loud in the passageway outside. "I want to see her! Now!"

This wasn't quite what I had planned, but his arrival saved me a trip.

He saw me when I left his father's bedroom, dismissing the guard blocking his entrance to fire a salvo my way.

"Are you completely stupid?" he shouted, anger behind every word. "You arrested my father? My lawyers are already set to meet the ship in New York. When we have finished suing the cruise line for your incompetence, we will raise a personal case against you …"

I lifted my hands, palms out, begging him to calm down.

"Who would want to frame your father?"

My question caught Tim by surprise, spoiling whatever he was going to say next. He blinked and gave a little shake to reset his head.

I cut him off before he got a chance to ask a question. "We need to talk."

He was still in the passageway, the Ensign on the door doing his job. I joined him, taking hold of his unresisting arm which I tugged to make him come with me.

Tim didn't fight me, but he sure had some questions.

"If you think my father is being framed, why have you locked him up? You can't treat him like a criminal and get away with it, Mrs Fisher. Who do you suspect? Why are they doing it? Are they after money? Is there some kind of demand? What makes you think my father is being framed?"

I wasn't going to get into it in the passageway. Equally, I didn't want to travel all the way down to my team's base on deck ten to conduct an interview. Rooting through my handbag, I found the universal door card I keep and swiped at a maintenance door. Every deck has them.

Hoping I wouldn't find crew performing some routine task on the other side, I was relieved to receive no response to my request of, "Is anyone in here?"

"What are we doing in here, Mrs Fisher?" The questions just kept coming.

I noted Tim's choice to return to addressing me formally. I had been Patricia for weeks since we got to know each other.

FOUR EX-WIVES AND A WEDDING

Closing the door and turning to face him in the cramped space, I said, "We are attempting to get to the bottom of what is going on, Tim. There are no sides to this, so I am not on your side. Or anyone else's for that matter. Operating in my capacity as the ship's detective, my sole aim is to uncover the truth and make sure the person or people behind the crimes are held to account."

I waited to see if Tim was going to argue or barrage me with another deluge of questions. When he didn't, I continued.

"Very well. Your father is under arrest and currently in the brig because I have overwhelming evidence against him." Tim sucked in a breath to start arguing and I stopped him with a hand in the air. "Please let me continue. The murder weapon has been found in his suite, he had your mother's blood on his shirt," a tricky subject to throw in Tim's face, "and he has no alibi for the times when the murders took place …"

"I didn't know any of that." Tim's voice was quiet when he spoke and it was clear he was not only stunned by what I was telling him, but deeply worried by it. "But you said he is being framed?" he added more brightly.

"Possibly. Your mother threatened your father yesterday."

Tim's forehead creased with a deep frown. "She did what? Threatened him how?"

"She demanded he call off the wedding and he was going to do it."

Tim's confusion continued to deepen. "Hold on. You just said she threatened him."

"Yes, with something unspoken. Your mother held a secret your father wanted her to keep so badly he was prepared to call off the wedding. Tim, I need to know what it was."

His eyes widened, the question being posed sinking in.

"I don't know. Honestly, Patricia, I was two when my parents split up. If there is some big secret then I'm afraid I don't know what it is."

I believed him. I wasn't happy about it, but it sounded like the truth. While I took a moment to ponder the ramifications of his answer, he went back to asking questions.

"What does this have to do with someone trying to frame my father?"

I could only offer a shrug, but doing so would make me look less in control or less professional maybe. Whichever it was, I chose to provide an alternative response.

"At this time, I cannot say. What I can tell you is that your father had reason to want your mother out of the picture." Tim drew a breath to argue once more and I rode right over the top of him. "Whatever the secret is, I believe it died with your mother. Now only your father knows, and he refuses to talk."

"Let me speak with him."

"I'm afraid not. Not yet, Tim. Let's put the secret to one side for now and focus on who might want to frame your father for two murders."

"My father didn't kill anyone."

"Yes, that may be the case, but the evidence is sufficient to convict him, please believe me. Who stands to gain, Tim?"

An unhappy chuckle escaped him. "Who stands to gain? Our competitors for sure. Stock dropped ten points last night after that Hollywood gossip monger broadcast my father's face and asked him if he paid to have my mother killed or did it himself."

"The Mouth?" I questioned, sure I had the name right.

"That's him, scummy little bottom feeder preying on everyone else's indiscretions. I wonder what would come tumbling out if someone were to shine a spotlight on his private life."

Pushing the unpleasant media hound to one side to focus on the previous question, I posed it a different way.

"Who stands to gain the most, Tim? If someone is behind this, and I hope they are - your father is a sweet old man," my admission got a nod of acknowledgement, "then they have gone to a lot of trouble to make it look like your father is the killer."

Tim simply didn't have anything to tell me. We went around and around the subject for a few minutes, but he was unable to shed any light on the situation.

"You're going to release him now, yes?"

"I cannot do that, Tim. He is the prime ... the only suspect in a double homicide." Tim was going to fight me until I presented an angle he'd not considered. "Imagine you are the killer and your sole aim is to frame John Oswald. If he is locked up, you cannot strike again. To do so would throw everything into question. However ..."

Tim sagged. "If you let him out, they might kill again. Can't you put an armed guard on him? Won't that ensure he cannot be connected to another crime. Won't that keep everyone safe?"

"I can't risk it, Tim. We can't risk it. Your father had an armed guard on him yesterday in the form of one of my officers. That didn't stop him making his own way back through the ship when the rehearsal dinner had to be scrapped."

"Where was your security officer?"

"She wasn't required to watch him during the dinner and that was supposed to last hours. I pulled her away to help me interview your father's other ex-wives."

Tim's lip curled. "Now there's a gang of suspects right there. They hated my mother and they would happily see my father go to jail."

"Yes, but one of them was murdered last night, Tim."

Yet again I hit Tim with a startling revelation and this time the news made him jolt.

"What! Who? Which one?"

"Fiona," I made my voice quiet to deliver the answer.

Tim sagged against the bulkhead, his head down for a moment. When he looked up, he said, "Sorry, I've just realised you said two murders. You said that more than once, in fact. I didn't really hear it until just now."

Sympathising with the man – his mother was murdered less than a day ago – I placed a hand on his arm.

"Carol and Imelda were confined to their cabins with guards on the door. Whoever is behind this, it isn't them." Which was annoying because the ex-wives were my prime suspects until an hour ago.

"What are you going to do, Patricia? I refuse to have my father held in a jail cell for a crime he did not commit."

What was I going to do? How I wish I had an answer to that question. Right now it felt like my only option was to clutch at straws. Wine glasses with holes in, murdered ex-wives, overwhelming evidence that had to have been placed so it would be found, and on top of all that Lady Mary's scruffy man.

Where did he fit into all this?

One Crime Solved

A call from Lieutenant Pippin provided a breakthrough in the ex-wives wedding sabotage plans. He was still in Fiona's cabin with the team collating evidence. Fiona's body was gone, on its way to the morgue.

"Mrs Fisher." I got a nod of greeting upon arrival back at the most recent crime scene.

Stepping inside the suite, I knew what to expect and went straight to Pippin.

"A dentist drill?" My face screwed up in disbelief.

"I found it in a bag, Mrs Fisher," announced Sam with a goofy grin.

I had to hold it away from my face to be able to focus on the tiny drill tip, but there was no doubt in my mind I was looking at the device used to make the holes in the wine glasses. It all came back to the ex-wives. Cakes with threatening messages, firecrackers that never got to go off, wine glasses with holes in ... who knew what other tricks we were yet to uncover or had been planned but never executed.

Standing next to me as I examined the minute drill, Pippin said, "Her husband is a Beverly Hills dentist. He owns a string of practices and boasts A-lister clients like Channing Tatum and Sandra Bullock. It was easy to find the information once I knew what to look for."

Okay, so it was nothing to do with the double homicide, but short on leads to follow, it felt good to have something I could do.

Carrying the dentist drill in an evidence bag, I made my way to the security team outpost on deck nineteen. They had a room there I could use and the two remaining ex-wives were being brought to me. They had been made aware of Fiona's murder more than an hour ago and left to stew – a cruel tactic possibly, but not one I was about to regret.

I stayed out of the way when they were escorted inside and refused to make eye contact with Imelda though I could feel her glare on the back of my head.

When I joined them, I did so with Lieutenants Bhukari and Schneider either side of me. I was done being stonewalled and was out to intimidate.

The old tactic of remaining silent to see if they would confess their sins hadn't worked before and it didn't work now either. Their expressions were close to unreadable but there was joy in their eyes – they thought they had won.

"You do not seem all that upset about Fiona," I observed as a prompt to get someone talking.

Imelda gave a one shoulder shrug. "Should we be?"

"Wasn't she part of your little conspiracy? Or are you so cutthroat you just don't care that she was stabbed through the heart last night."

Cold as ice, Imelda said nothing, but I saw Carol's lip wobble.

"Still convinced we are behind the supposed sabotage to the rehearsal dinner?" scoffed Imelda. "How could we have done such a thing when we were locked in our cabins."

I lifted the evidence bag from the deck and placed it on the table between us.

"This is Fiona's. Or more accurately, her husband's. She used it to drill the holes in the wine glasses and could have pulled that off long before the guests assembled for the dinner. I tested the drill on a wine glass, it went through like warm butter. She could have made all those holes in less than ten minutes." I swung my gaze to glare at Carol. "You set firecrackers to go off in the banquet room and you sent your grandson to deliver a cake to Betty Ross."

Carol said nothing and refused to meet my eyes. As usual it was Imelda who spoke.

"You can't prove anything and even if you could, it no longer matters. Even if you were able to convince a judge to charge us, the wedding is off, and our future is secure. John is locked up and can no longer ruin the company we all have shares in."

"So that's it?" I finally got to the crux of it. "You were worried about your revenue stream?"

Imelda chuckled. "Wouldn't you be? We are talking about millions in dividends every year. It's not cheap to look this good." She wafted a hand at her face. "That blonde bimbo and her awful family would have embarrassed the firm and goodness knows how much they might have spent before John did the decent thing and died."

Imelda was such a delight to spend time with.

"John killed Lexington," she continued, "and I, for one, don't blame him. She was a loathsome woman. Ultimately, his arrest means the company will fall to Tim to run and he is a worthy successor. We have been encouraging John to stand down for years. So, good luck making anything stick to us," Imelda finished triumphantly; a broad, satisfied grin spreading across her face.

I took my time and relished wiping it off.

"There's just one rather important factor you appear to have overlooked."

"Nonsense," Imelda laughed in my face.

"John didn't kill anyone."

Imelda's smile froze and Carol jolted as if stuck with an electric probe.

"What do you mean?" Carol asked, speaking for the first time. "Yes, he did. We heard he was arrested for it."

Imelda's nose had wrinkled. Looking down it at me like I was something she might have trodden in, she said, "What is this? Who else would have killed Lexie? Or Fiona? Of course it was John."

I shook my head. "No, he's being framed." While the theory fit in my head, I had been far from sure about it, but saying it aloud now, using it as a weapon against his ex-wives, I believed I had it right. "Someone else killed Lexington Brand and Fiona Sugarman. The killer wants John to suffer the indignity of jail. I'm about to release him from the brig. I'm afraid the wedding is very much back on and I wonder which of you the killer might decide to target next. Or maybe it won't be one of you, but let's face it, you came gunning for John, so if the killer wants a credible target …"

"Okay, it was us!" wailed Carol.

Imelda shot daggers from her eyes. "Shhhhh, Carol! What has gotten into you?"

"Enough is enough, Imelda!" Carol had tears running down her cheeks. "I believe her! I never pegged John as a murderer. He would have killed me when I left him if he was that kind of person." She aimed an imploring gaze in my direction. "I want protection. Please. It was me, okay? When my son, Roger, found out about the wedding, I knew we had to put a stop to it. I contacted Fiona and Imelda. I even contacted Lexie, but she said she already knew from Tim. We believed that if we ruined the event, it wouldn't go ahead."

Imelda, fuming at Carol's lack of backbone wasn't going to let anyone else have the last word.

"I doubt it matters. From what I hear, the bride's family have been robbing the wedding guests. John won't walk down the aisle with the daughter of a thief no matter how besotted he is."

Shocking News

"So you're letting John Oswald go?" Lieutenant Deepa Bhukari wanted to confirm moments later when we were outside the interview room. "Should I contact the guys in the brig?"

My hands were gripping the sides of my head. What the heck was I supposed to do now? I couldn't let John out and I couldn't keep him in.

I had solved one of the three cases hanging over my head and felt confident the ex-wives were not going to attempt any further mischief. Once I had given myself time to think and was confident I had no further questions for them, they would be returned to their cabins under guard.

That decision led me neatly to the next question I wanted answered: who was guarding Fiona's door around the time when she was murdered? I knew it was going to be two people because she died between ten-thirty and midnight. It could be no earlier than that because she was still being interviewed by me.

"Patricia?" Deepa prompted me to give an answer.

"What? Oh, sorry, yes. I mean no. I, um ... I think we should hang on."

That Deepa's face bore a confused look was not surprising.

I was thinking fast. I didn't want to let John out, but I did want to make the killer think I had. Was that safe? I had no idea who the killer could be and what if they struck again? It would prove John was indeed innocent, but at the cost of another life. That wasn't a gamble I could take.

Usually, when I am on the right path I get a little itch at the back of my skull. I couldn't tell you what it is or where it comes from, only that I have learned to interpret and follow it and that it was conspicuously absent today.

"So, what do we do?" Deepa wanted to know.

"Has Martin rounded up whoever was guarding Mrs Sugarman's door last night?"

Deepa didn't know but was on her radio a second later finding out. Frustrated by my lack of progress, I called Barbie for an update.

"We might have something," she was hesitant to reveal, the absence of confidence in her voice doing nothing to instil me with hope. "We focused on anything that happened when John and Lexie were married. I figured if it is something powerful that only she knows, it must have gone down when they were together."

"That makes sense," I replied, wishing she would get to the point.

"You may want to come and see it. We are still exploring to see if this is something or nothing."

"Ok, but what is it?" I begged, my tone exasperated.

Barbie giggled in my ear. "See, Patty? It's not fun when one person knows the answer and won't tell anyone, is it?"

She was getting her own back. The way my brain works is that the answers just sort of appear when I have seen enough clues. Having the answer doesn't always solve the crime though. Sometimes, to be sure you are able to get the confession or catch the perpetrator in the act, you need to lead them into revealing themselves. I come up with, admittedly, strange plans to make that happen all too regularly, but never tell my friends quite what

I have arranged in my head because I'm still figuring it out and don't want to tell them that. Plus, it's fun to watch them squirm, just like Barbie was doing to me now.

"Please, Barbie," I begged.

"Okay, so here it is: I think John killed someone."

As headlines go, that was the kind that jumped off the page and punched you in the teeth when you weren't looking.

Brain now racing, I murmured something like, "I'll be right there," and ended the call.

Deepa caught sight of the look on my face. "Everything okay? Martin has Ensign Roach and Lieutenant Gallagher waiting for you. Should I say you are on your way?"

I bit my lip and made an on-the-spot decision. "No, please ask him to wait. I need to check on something else first." I twitched toward the door, intended to go, but spun back around to face Deepa. "Actually, you might want to come with me."

Schneider shot a look, asking a question.

"Please escort the ex-wives back to their cabins and have them confined there."

He seemed surprised. "You're not charging them?"

"Not yet." Honestly, I didn't feel I had time to give the question the thought it required. "They can stay in their cabins until we reach New York. They will be ejected there and banned from future cruises. Beyond that, there isn't much to gain. Betty and John can decide if they wish to raise a civil lawsuit. I'll think on it though so please make it clear they are not out of trouble yet."

Too eager to learn more from Barbie, I left Lieutenant Schneider to get on with it and raced out the door with Deepa on my heels.

Cold Case

My suite was quiet save for the sound of the dogs barking to repel the intruders when I opened the door. Realising it was me, they calmed and danced around my feet until I fussed them.

Jermaine, still in his butler's livery, closed the door and took Deepa's hat, giving it a brush before placing it on a shelf in the lobby.

Barbie was at the desk, a large oak thing inlaid with a leather pad for writing. Not that I did much actual writing, and it was currently obscured by two laptops set side by side for Barbie and Jermaine to work together.

"Ah, Patricia," said Lady Mary, closing the book she was reading. "Are you done for the day? I'm parched. Perhaps we could venture out for some elevenses?"

"It's nine thirty," I pointed out.

"Never too early to not be late, that's what I always say," she grinned and waited for my answer. She was here for John's wedding, but staying with me because we are friends. I hadn't really spent any time with her yet and she wanted to go for cocktails. I couldn't though. Not yet.

"Sorry, Mary. If I can close this case, I promise you, me, Felicity, and whoever wants to join us will hit one of the cocktail bars and drink it dry."

"Now that sounds more like it. Are you getting any closer to finding the killer?" she enquired hopefully.

I swung my attention to Barbie hunched over her laptop.

"Are we?"

Just like I claimed she would, the Californian blonde, internet ninja had found an obscure thread. It related to a death fifty-eight years ago. Barbie found it almost by accident.

Researching John's career and life specifically during the time he was married to Lexie got them nowhere. It was only when Jermaine suggested looking at the time running up to their marriage – the year or so when they would have been dating – that she struck gold.

John made millions by the time he was twenty-one - his portfolio of firms defied belief. He'd moved to L.A. where he schmoozed with the hot people because he had money. That was how he got into funding films and being associated with the film industry. Until Barbie started showing me pictures of him with Hollywood stars, a different starlet on his arm every time, I had no idea how deeply entrenched he was in that life.

He met and married Lexington, but just weeks before they tied the knot, one of John's many companies, something called Obsequious Design, ceased to exist. Curious to know what might have happened, Barbie dug into the details of the business.

It's a fortunate thing that company records are public – at least at a basic level, because there Barbie found the name of John's business partner: Alex Schmidt. Only seconds after that she discovered he was dead. Not recently, but right when the company went down the drain.

Alex Schmidt was survived by a wife and son. However, other than names, Barbie had been unable to learn anything of use about what had become of them.

All the money seemingly vanished overnight two days before Alex died. There were a few small news snippets about the firm closing unexpectedly, but the bigger story was the way Alex Schmidt died.

He was shot in the head and though there was gunpowder residue on his right hand to suggest a suicide, the weapon itself was never found.

Pushing back from the desk, Barbie stretched in place. "If you are looking for a big secret Lexington Brand could hold over John Oswald's head, how about murder?"

It was all there. It was completely circumstantial and clearly the police at the time found too little evidence of anything to pursue a conviction. Nevertheless, one had to admit that it fit.

"You found nothing else?" I asked.

Barbie shook her head. "Not so far. That doesn't mean it isn't out there, but I've only been on it for an hour."

To believe John might have killed his partner was easy, but it also required a leap. Nothing Barbie found suggested there was any reason why John would want his partner dead. Their business – supplying costumes to Hollywood film producers - appeared to be thriving which begged the question: why shut it down?

Running some ideas through my head, I said, "Let's assume this is something. It's almost sixty years ago so who would choose now to come after John?"

Deepa asked, "What about the kid? He would be in his sixties or seventies now, I guess. Could the murders be an elaborate revenge tactic intended to finally send John Oswald to jail? If you are right about this being a frame, but if he went to jail for the murders of Lexington and Fiona, then he could be perceived as finally paying for the murder of Alex Schmidt."

Barbie pulled up her notes. "The son was seven when it happened making him sixty-five now. His name is Reuben."

"Like the sandwich?" I asked, suddenly hungry.

Barbie sniggered, but confirmed I was right. I only asked because I had never met or even heard of a person called Reuben. That's about my lack of worldliness and nothing else. It just struck me as odd in the moment. A bit like naming a person 'cheese and pickle'.

I grabbed an apple from a fruit bowl and bit into it – significantly healthier than a sandwich though far less satisfying.

Pausing between bites, I asked, "Mary, how old would you say your Scruffy man was?"

Her eyebrows wiggled a little as she thought. With a shrug she said, "Late fifties would be my guess but everyone ages differently. He could be in his sixties, for sure."

Deepa was on her radio a heartbeat later, upping the priority to find the mysterious man.

Working the problem from a new angle, I said, "Mary, I need you to look through some passenger photographs on central registry."

She squinted at me. "How many?"

"However many white men fall into the age band."

"That sounds like hundreds and hundreds."

I made an apologetic face. "It might really help."

Lady Mary exhaled through her lips, ruffling them in her resigned acceptance. "There had better be some gin involved in this task."

I was leaving, that much I knew. Touching Barbie on the arm, I asked, "Can you stay on it? See what else you can find?"

Barbie kicked with her feet to push the chair back to the desk.

"Sure thing. This is fun. Almost as good as press-ups."

Deepa asked, "Aren't you supposed to be back in the gym already? Your ankle seems fine."

"It is," she agreed. "More or less. I never stopped in the gym though. I can reduce a class to a sweaty, tearful mess on one leg. Tony is covering my class this morning though, so I'm all good here for a few more hours."

"Come on, girls," I called to the dogs and clapped my hands. Their little heads popped up instantly, making sure I meant them before bouncing down to the deck. They nipped at each other in their excitement.

Leaving Barbie and Jermaine behind, I took Deepa with me once again as this time I set off for the brig.

"Time to quiz Mr Oswald?" she asked.

"Time to get some answers." I could feel the determined set to my jaw. There was a killer on board my ship and maybe John knew who it was. Maybe he didn't; I favoured the latter, but he knew something and I was going to squeeze it out of him. I only hoped the big secret Lexie threatened him with was the one Barbie uncovered. If not, I was still at square one.

A Haunting Truth

The dachshunds led the way as they always do, dragging me in whichever direction I sent them. To get to the brig from my suite is a simple enough route but involves more than one elevator as almost all of them stop at deck seven so the passengers cannot access the crew levels. The bottom six decks are filled with the ship's engines, fresh water tanks, storage spaces, a vault, the sickbay, the brig, lots more, and of course the crew accommodation.

When I set off, I took a winding route to give the girls some fresh air on the sundeck so the journey from A to B took almost half an hour, about five minutes longer than it otherwise might. I was in a hurry, but my dogs still need to be exercised.

Deepa had radioed ahead so the officers manning the brig knew we were coming.

Greeted at the door, Lieutenant Ickenroth, an Austrian, said, "Mrs Fisher, your suspect is already in the interview room for you."

I thanked him, left my dachshunds with the two chaps working in the brig today, and led Deepa into the small room where John sat staring at the wall.

His usual vibrancy and energy were missing as though the mere process of incarceration had stripped them from his body. It had only been a couple of hours, but the billionaire looked sunken and withdrawn. It was not the first time I'd seen this effect. Left in silence to stew over their increasingly bleak future, a suspect can find their past arrives to eat away their soul.

"Have you come to let me out?" John growled, showing me he was far from beaten by his situation.

I took my time, settling into the chair opposite. The table could accommodate four – two either side - or six, I suppose if you stuck one more on each end and people didn't mind their knees touching.

Deepa sat next to me, a Dictaphone ready to record everything being said and a notepad so she could take notes.

Meeting John's eyes, I said, "No. I am here for information, John. However, I hope to be able to release you soon. Whether I can or not depends entirely on you."

He made a small scoffing noise and kept his eyes boring into mine.

"What happened to Alex Schmidt and Obsequious Design?" My question was intended to shock the man opposite. If I was right, that is. If I was way off the mark, I doubted he would react at all.

"How?" John tried to hide his change in facial expression, but not quickly enough. He looked down, seemed to argue with himself for a moment, then looked back up with a resigned set to his face and posture. "How much do you know?"

I could bluff and pretend I knew it all, stringing him along to tease more and more of the truth from the one person who knew it, but something about the way he asked made me choose the truth instead.

"Nothing really, John, but I have people looking into it now. I know you were partners with Alex. I know the money vanished and just a couple of days later Alex was killed with a single bullet to the head. This was weeks before you got married for the first time and I believe the truth about what happened was the thing Lexington held over you. Did you kill him?"

John reacted as if slapped. "What? No, I didn't kill Alex! So far as I know he killed himself."

"They never found the gun. How do you explain that if it was suicide?"

John shook his head and shrugged, but said, "Look the police questioned me at the time. I was out to dinner with Lexington. We were seen by dozens of people. If someone did kill Alex, it wasn't me. What happened to the gun is anyone's guess, but he was found at a building site. I think he went there to kill himself rather than do it at home and have his boy, Reuben, find him. The gun could have been picked up by a vagrant and pawned, I just don't know and no one ever will."

I had to stay on my toes just to keep up with the developing story in my head.

"So, if you didn't kill Alex, what was so terrible that Lexington was able to hold it over you? What is worse than murder?"

John looked positively sick and the fierce, dominant attitude that made him a billionaire was nowhere in sight. Refusing to meet my eyes, he released a long sigh, his shoulders dropping two inches as he deflated.

Finally, he started to talk.

"I had other business interests, you understand. I let Alex run Obsequious Designs while I did all the glad-handing and client meets. I was the power-lunch part of the business, the one who sold it. Alex produced the goods."

"So what went wrong? Tell me something John because this is getting us nowhere. Who murdered Lexington and Fiona?"

He didn't answer my question, but continued with his story as if I hadn't spoken.

"We were making millions. I didn't notice at first and I take full responsibility for my lack of oversight."

I frowned, unsure what he was trying to say.

"It was all illegal," he revealed with another deep sigh. "Alex told me the factory was efficient and could produce costumes not only fast but at a rate far below any of the competitors. I should have known something was wrong, but in more than a year of trading, I never once made the time to visit the factory. You know, I don't recall it even occurring to me."

Deepa was scribbling notes next to me, her hand moving fast to keep up.

"Eventually, it was the numbers that tipped me off. There was no way we could make the money we were. It was as if we had no overhead costs or were paying the staff nothing for their labours."

A little itch at the back of my skull provided the answer before he could say it.

"Alex had a series of sweatshops using illegal immigrants smuggled across the Mexican border. They came voluntarily with the promise of a new life only to find themselves held captive and subjected to terrible working and living conditions. I was getting rich, and I had no idea people were suffering for my fortune."

Nearly six decades had passed and the man still looked and sounded ashamed and horrified. Under any other circumstances I would have reached out to place a hand on his arm in comfort. Too worried I might break the spell, I didn't move a muscle.

"I confronted Alex and he laughed at me. He scoffed that it was too late to stop now. We had contracts to fulfil and were anyone to ever find out, we would both go to jail."

This would be the point where ordinarily I would expect a suspect to admit he killed the other person – right after justifying it was necessary. However, that's not John's story.

"I cleaned out the business account that day. I had full access to it, so I withdrew every penny and I went to the sweatshops. The people were being held under armed guard and they were terrified." John looked up to meet my eyes, the pain in his face manifesting in tears that swam in his eyes, threatening to fall. "I know I should have called the cops. I should have blown the whole thing open and faced the consequences, but Lexington was pregnant. It was less than a week since she told me and my whole world felt like it was balancing on a precipice. So I protected myself. I protected my family."

"What did you do?" I couldn't help myself; I was completely absorbed by his story.

"I paid the guards off. I paid for their silence. Then I freed all the immigrants. The money from the business and more from my own pocket went into their hands in the form of ten thousand dollars cash each. It was a lot of money back then. Enough to give them options. If I'd called the police, they would have all been deported and arrived back in Mexico penniless. Instead, I gave them opportunity and I like to think they are still here, thriving with their children and grandchildren. I'm not trying to sell myself as the hero in this situation. I'm not. My negligence … my willingness to be fooled cost those people dearly and I should have done more. I should probably still be doing more, but I sent them on their way without once considering how I might contact them to make sure they were okay."

John lapsed into silence, a single tear running down his left cheek.

Casting my gaze to the right, I found Deepa looking back at me, a matching tear running down her face. It was quite the story.

John had done as close to the right thing as he could at the time without exposing himself and his family to investigation and all the horror that would have come with the truth being aired. It had haunted him ever since.

Now though, were the truth to come out, it would damage his reputation and stain everything his firm and his family stood for. Stock would crash, people would lose their jobs … no wonder he wanted Lexington to keep it secret.

But there it was. Everything came back to Lexington and who killed her and then Fiona. If not John, then who?

A knock at the door drew my attention, Deepa moving faster than me to step outside and see who wanted what.

A moment later, she popped her head back around the door. "Mrs Fisher. I have Barbie on the phone."

Believing I might need to speak with John again, depending on what Barbie might have to tell me, I left him in the interview room.

Knowing I was heading for the brig, Barbie used the ship's internal phone system to contact me. Lieutenant Ickenroth had the phone in his hand, holding it out for me to take.

"Barbie? Did Lady Mary identify the scruffy man?"

"Oh, ah, no, sorry. Not yet anyways. That doesn't matter though because I know who the killer is."

And the Killer is ...

Deepa and I all but sprinted back to my suite. With Barbie's big reveal ringing in my ears, the biggest question I had was why the back of my skull hadn't itched when I heard the name.

About halfway from one place to the other, it occurred to me that I probably should have asked John why he hadn't said anything. Surely he knew. But then again, maybe he didn't. It was all so long ago.

The dachshunds tore along in front of me like mad things, their leads short for the trip hazard it created. Nevertheless, I must have apologised twenty times as they wove between people and almost caused me to collide with passengers happily minding their own business.

Out of breath, we arrived back at my suite. Why the hurry to get there? Because I wanted to see the evidence for myself.

Lady Mary had a glass of gin in each hand; one of which she was sipping from, the other she offered to me. It was almost eleven o'clock.

"No, thank you, Mary."

"Oh, thank goodness," she replied, placing the first glass on a table and diving straight into the second. "Staring at pictures is thirsty work."

"Still no luck?"

She shook her head. "A little Dunkirk spirit will see the task to its conclusion. I just needed a quick break to refresh my palate."

Jermaine took the dogs, releasing them from their collars and stowing their leads. They shot off across the cabin to their water bowl and I went to Barbie at the computer.

She angled away, moving the chair back so I could get close to the screen.

"It's all there. Reuben Schmidt's mother remarried five years after his father died and changed their name to Horowitz. Reuben married at twenty-seven producing five children with his wife, Alice. The youngest son they named Reuben Horowitz Junior."

I would have not the faintest idea what significance that held had Barbie not already told me.

Reuben Horowitz Junior was no name for a person in the spotlight. It was too much of a mouthful, especially when it could be substituted for something far catchier and more memorable like The Mouth.

The grandson of Alex Schmidt, the man who died as a result of John's decision to close their business grown from the tears of peoples' suffering, was on the ship and had already shown his hand. According to Barbie, The Mouth taunted John at the rehearsal dinner, asking him if he paid someone to kill Lexington or had the guts to do it himself.

The Mouth knew neither thing was true because he killed her. He then killed Fiona when I failed to incarcerate John following the first murder.

Or did he?

It sounded right. The Schmidts had fallen into poverty after Alex killed himself. All the money went away and for the wife and son it must have seemed as though John Oswald was the man behind their ruination.

Possibly, Reuben even believed John was responsible for his father's death. Sure, John had an alibi, but would a person overwhelmed with grief and anger care about such a thing?

Despite that, I couldn't quite make the dots connect in my head.

My radio crackled, Martin's voice booming out of my handbag.

"Lieutenant Commander Baker for Mrs Fisher, over."

"This is Mrs Fisher, over."

He still had the two men waiting to be interviewed about how someone got past them last night. I needed an answer, but it still hadn't reached the top of the priority list.

"Can you dismiss them for now?" I asked, "And come to my suite? There has been a development. In fact, please assemble the whole team, over."

Barbie eyed me suspiciously. "You're up to something, Patty. You are wearing your devious look."

"No, I'm not," I argued, darting to check my face in the mirror by the door in case I was. Did I have a devious face?

When I turned around to face the room again, every person in it was looking at me with the same single raised eyebrow – they all thought Barbie was right. It was a conspiracy.

Making my face as emotionless as I could, I said, "I'm not being devious, I'm thinking about how we can catch a killer."

The door behind me beeped quietly, as someone outside operated the lock. I twisted to see Mindy coming through it with Felicity.

"Never again," complained Mindy. "Never again will I say organising a wedding on a cruise ship is a good idea. We should stay at home and use the people we know."

Felicity looked like she agreed, and it made me cringe a little.

"Some problems cancelling the suppliers and standing everyone down?" I asked innocently.

Felicity spotted Lady Mary's drink. Pointing at it, she asked, "Is there more where that came from?" Apparently, it was a day for pre-lunch drinks. While Jermaine mixed her a gin and tonic, Felicity flopped into a chair. "Mindy is not wrong about it being easier at home where we are a known commodity. I have had irate New Yorkers in my ears for the last three hours."

"The guests weren't exactly fun either," said Mindy.

Felicity sighed. "No, quite a few acted as though it was our decision to stop the wedding. They all have busy lives and too much to do to have me waste their precious time bringing them to a wedding that fails to take place."

I raised a hand to interrupt the moaning.

"Um."

Felicity looked at me, her face questioning for a few seconds before she guessed what I wanted to say.

"Don't you dare, Patricia Fisher. Don't you dare tell me the wedding is back on!"

I made a cringing face. "Does it help if I'm reeeeally sorry?"

Mindy tensed her body, tipped back her head, and yelled her frustration. "I hate cruise ship weddings!"

Felicity clasped her hands to her face aghast. "What changed? When we left here you were locking the groom up for a double homicide."

"Yes." I turned to face Deepa. "Can you please arrange to have John released from the brig. I think I had better speak to Alistair and explain what is going on."

Lady Mary raised a hand. "What *is* going on? Or am I the only one in the dark?"

Bait and Lure

I met Alistair in the passageway outside John's suite. I could have met John by myself, but the captain of the ship – a more prominent representative of Purple Star Cruise Lines – was the right man to smooth the ripples from this particular pond.

Lieutenant Commander Baker, understanding the gravity and complexity of the situation, went to the brig himself to fetch John Oswald. Once John Oswald was safely back in his accommodation, Alistair and I chose to visit.

It was not the case that we had done the groom a disservice; I had acted entirely as the situation demanded. However, locking an eighty-two-year-old man away for murder on the eve of his wedding only to subsequently determine his innocence was not something that could go without comment.

Prepared to ride a barrage of contempt from both John and his eldest son, Tim, I was immensely relieved to find them both pleased to see me.

Not so much when I refused to divulge the name of the new suspect.

"What do you mean you won't tell us?" demanded Tim. "We have a right to know! What if the killer targets someone else now? That's what you said you feared earlier."

"That was before I knew who to watch, Tim. The suspect is being monitored closely and carefully by a dozen of the ship's security officers. I believe this is the best tactic if we want to catch them." I was careful to keep my pronouns neutral.

"Why can't you just arrest whoever it is?" asked John. He was sitting in an armchair with a stiff bourbon warming in his hand.

"No evidence. What I have is circumstantial at best. The knife had no fingerprints on it and while DNA testing may reveal a connection it won't be enough. I cannot place the suspect at either crime scene or provide motivation for their crimes other than the desire to frame you, John. If I arrest them now, the risk they might walk free is too great."

"So what are you proposing?" Tim demanded, anger evident in his tone. "That you use the wedding and its guests as what … some sort of lure to trap the killer? That's it isn't it? You think the killer will try to strike again."

I nodded grimly. "Yes. That is my hope. That is why I have taken Imelda and Carol out of protective custody. They are being watched too."

John snorted his disbelief. "How did you get them to agree to that?"

"I gave them very little choice." Honestly, I gave them no choice at all. They were guilty of all sorts of things and though I didn't plan to charge them, they didn't need to know that.

Tim had more arguments to raise, but his father got in first. "What do you need us to do?"

John agreed to just act naturally. With five hundred guests on board for his wedding, people were going to ask him how it was that he was suddenly free again. He would tell them his arrest was a ruse intended to draw the real killer out and that a person was currently locked in the brig.

He was leaving his suite in the next few minutes to visit Betty. She was yet to be informed the wedding was back on but we all agreed it was best coming from John.

Now that we were back on the subject of his father's imminent nuptials, Tim asked, "What about her family, dad? How can you overlook that they have been stealing from everyone? From what I hear, some of your guests are threatening to boycott the ceremony and the reception if you allow them to attend."

"I can hardly deny them access, son. They are Betty's only family. There are five hundred guests attending and only ten of them are here for the bride. That's a cruel enough statistic to start with."

Tim gave me an imploring look. "You're the ship's detective, Mrs Fisher. Surely it's your remit to stop them robbing people and make them return what they have taken."

He made a fair point, and though I wanted to point out that I had been really rather busy with the double homicide and proving his father's innocence, to do so would be petty and sound too much like I was making excuses.

To avoid that, I said, "I will make it a priority."

Leaving the Platinum Suite a few moments later, I thanked Alistair for being there.

He pulled me into a kiss. The kind of kiss that makes me close my eyes. When he broke away, he had a question for me.

"Do you really think you can do this without anyone getting hurt?"

I didn't think that was a fair thing to ask, but I said, "Yes, or I would not be doing it. Lieutenant Commander Baker and the others will be diligent in their duties, you can have no fear of that. I cannot, however, predict the result."

Alistair accepted my answer and asked if he could escort me to my next destination.

I thanked him, but I had to speak with the Ross family now and it was better if he distanced himself from the conversation about to ensue.

Mystery Guest

"No one 'ing stole anything," insisted Betty's mother, Helen. "Just like yesterday, we are all totally 'ing innocent."

One of the worst parts about my job is that one quickly learns how dishonest the average person can be. They will lie to your face while emptying your pocket and feel not one shred of remorse or guilt for doing so.

The evidence was stacked against Mrs Ross yesterday, but I gave her the benefit of the doubt. Partly that was because of why she was on board – arresting her would have been terribly embarrassing for John and Betty – but also because the top in her bag was circumstantial. Oh, I could have charged her, for sure … I mean, how else could it have found its way into her bag unless she put it there. There was room for argument though, so I let it go. Now I regretted that decision.

"Mrs Ross," I continued. "I'm afraid there are multiple complaints of items … luxury items such as designer purses, expensive tablets, and suchlike going missing whenever your family are around. I cannot ignore them."

"So what are you 'ing saying?" asked Helen's sister Pauline. "You think we are a bunch of 'ing light-fingered tealeaves?"

Essentially, yes.

"That is not what I am saying," I lied. "However, the correlation cannot be ignored."

"Ooh, listen to her with her 'ing big words," Helen mugged to the family around her, jabbing a thumb in my direction. "I think it's time you left, Mrs High-and-Mighty. I'm not 'ing standing here and being 'ing accused of something I haven't 'ing done."

Already tired of fighting and aggravated by their attitude, I summoned a team to inspect their suites. The Ross family occupied two suites on deck nineteen – some of the plushest accommodation available on the whole ship. I believe John would have put them on the top deck, but it was fully booked.

Betty's relatives kicked off as I knew they would, complaining bitterly if one cared to decipher the words between the tirade of expletives. They moped in the passageway outside, refusing to move away and watching as though they knew we would find nothing.

Unfortunately, during the process, and probably because they were hanging around in the passageway, they attracted the attention of one of their victims, a teeny pop princess who had fire and attitude far beyond that which her size would suggest.

"There they are!" she accused, pointing at the Ross family and storming toward them.

One of Betty's younger siblings screamed her excitement.

"Oh, my God! It's Liberty Lace!"

"Yes, it's Liberty Lace!" yelled the popstrel. "It's Liberty Lace and she wants her phone back!"

The bigger problem was that young Miss Lace came with friends. And a boyfriend. As diminutive as she was, her boyfriend was the exact opposite. He made Tempest Michael's oversized friend, Big Ben, look average. Any taller and he would need to duck to walk down the passageways inside the ship.

"I want her phone back," he grumbled, his voice so deep I swear it emanated from the deck below.

"We haven't 'ing got it! All right?" Helen Ross shouted to add emphasis to a point she'd been making for some time.

"Yes, you have!" insisted Liberty. "Everyone knows you lot have been stealing from everyone."

As if on cue, more celebrities arrived and suddenly I had a brewing storm that needed to be deflected fast.

Sticking my head through the door of Helen's suite, I called out, "Has anyone found anything? Anything at all?"

"Of course they 'ing haven't!" yelled Helen upon hearing my question. It wasn't what I expected. Not even close, but I had to act upon the evidence I could see. Maybe they were savvy enough to stash the stolen phones and designer items somewhere I wouldn't think to look; somewhere not in their cabins. However they were doing it, I couldn't justify continuing to search their suites and needed to deal with the impending fight before it broke out.

Liberty was still demanding her phone back and Helen was taking out her earrings, a sure sign she planned to get physical if I didn't stop her.

I was going to get the ship's security officers out of their suites and the Ross family back inside. That would diffuse the situation, but turning around to start giving instruction I saw something ... someone who stopped me dead in my tracks.

"I believe I can shed some light on the current situation," said Detective Sergeant Mike Atwell.

"Mike?" I wanted to reach out and touch him to be sure he was real. "Mike what are you doing here?" I first met him a few months ago when I returned to England from my first cruise around the world. He and I ended up trying to solve the same cases from different angles and discovered we worked rather well together.

"We'll get to that," he said, turning toward Helen Ross who was just about to grab Liberty Lace by her tiny neck and was most likely going to get pummelled by the young pop star's boyfriend if she tried.

Stepping neatly into the gap between the two women, Mike said, "Oops, so sorry. Please excuse me. Hello. I know where your phone is, Miss Lace."

"Yeah!" she raged. "It's in this cow's cabin!"

Mike smiled congenially and blocked a wild slap Helen aimed at the smaller woman's face.

"Now, now. That will not help matters. I'm afraid you have been deceived, Miss Lace. Mrs Ross does not have your phone. Nor does she have anyone's possessions. The person behind these crimes lies elsewhere."

His calm demeanour and his soothing tone deescalated the situation just as much as the words he spoke.

Liberty's boyfriend, not coming across as particularly bright, nevertheless managed to ask the right question.

"So who is it?"

The security officers searching the Ross family's suites had come to join me in the passageway where everyone was now waiting on tenterhooks to hear Mike's big revelation.

With a knowing smile aimed at everyone, Mike said, "I think perhaps it will be better if I show you."

Seasoned Detective

On the way to wherever it was Mike was taking us, my phone rang with a call from Barbie.

"Babes, you are not going to believe who Lady Mary's scruffy man is!" she squealed in my ear.

"Is it Mike Atwell?"

I got stunned silence for several seconds, Barbie finally saying, "One day you are going to have to tell me how you do that. How could you possibly know that it's Mike?"

"Because he's walking next to me," I laughed.

Barbie gasped, "Did you sneak him on board again like you did when we were trying to catch the Godmother?"

"No. In fact, he's yet to tell me why he is here." Mike ground to halt in front of me, the procession of almost a hundred people following on behind bunching and pressing together to see why we had stopped. "Gotta go. I'll see you shortly, okay?"

I didn't hang on for Barbie's answer; Mike had turned around to address the crowd.

Directing a question at Liberty Lace, he asked, "What made you think Mrs Ross might have taken your phone, my dear?"

Liberty's ire had shrunk and more or less died in the period since we left the passageway outside Helen's cabin and when she spoke her voice was mousy, quiet, and distinctly less sure of itself.

"Well, it was someone at the party," she replied.

"You don't know his name?"

"No, but he said he saw … Mrs Ross," Liberty referred to Helen in a non-offensive manner for the first time, "snooping around my purse."

Helen, as usual, had something to say about that.

"Well, Missy, you need to get your 'ing facts straight before you start accusing people."

There was no need to comment and Mike didn't, choosing instead to address everyone else.

"Did anyone see Mrs Ross or any of her family take your possessions?"

I looked, rising onto my tiptoes to see the faces further back in the crowd but no one spoke. Except for whispered mutterings, that is.

I had a cringing feeling creeping up my spine. Like everyone else I was willing to believe the Ross family were guilty. It made me a bad person. A judgemental person. I'm not suggesting I had previously believed I was a perfect angel, yet throughout my life, the policy was always one of peace and harmony to all peoples. Somehow, in avoiding racism, homophobia, and bigotry of any kind, I had omitted to tackle classism.

My feet wanted to take me to Helen so I could apologise, but Mike was running the show and talking again.

"Final question: Does anyone know the name of the person who claimed to have seen Mrs Ross or a member of her family in the vicinity of your possessions?"

The answer came not from one person, but a whole bunch of them.

"Roger Oswald."

It seemed a goodly number of the wedding guests knew the person stirring the rumours.

Reaching out with one arm, Mike never took his eyes off the crowd filling the passageway when he rapped his knuckles smartly on a door. Until that moment, I thought he chose to stop randomly in a passageway, but that was not the case.

I've never met Roger Oswald, but when the cabin door opened and a man in his early fifties looked out, I could see John's features reflected in his face.

Pinned to the spot by the sea of faces looking directly at him, Roger froze, the colour draining from his face. He gave a yelp of fright and slammed the door shut.

At least, he tried to.

Mike had knocked on a few doors in his life and knew when to have a foot ready. His shoe jammed the door, the force with which Roger tried to close it causing it to bounce open again.

Roger backed away, terror filling his face.

Mike stalked into his room followed by me, Deepa, Helen Ross, and a host of others.

Liberty Lace was the first to raise her voice.

"Have you got my phone?"

Roger's guilty eyes twitched across to meet hers.

"Well? Have you? I want it back."

"S'right," said Liberty's hulking boyfriend. "She wants it back."

More demands filled the air as celebrities, family members, and more pushed into the nineteenth deck suite. Like everyone else in the Oswald family, Roger wasn't short of a penny, so the thefts had not been motivated by financial gain, celebrity envy, or even kleptomania. No, he took them to frame the Ross family.

It was a time for framing other people. I wondered if I had missed a memo.

Pushed inward by the surging crowd still trying to get into the suite – no one wanted to miss the action - Deepa chose to forge ahead. Crossing the room unnoticed by Roger, who had found his voice and was trying to protest his innocence, she started opening cupboards.

"Hey, what are you doing!" Roger jolted into action, racing to intercept Deepa as she opened the next cupboard in line. He might have got to her had Mike not 'accidentally' stuck his foot out.

Roger sprawled across the carpet, his face aimed at the cupboard like an arrow showing everyone the way when the door swung open and purses, phones, trinkets, and other personal items came tumbling out.

"Those are mine," Roger tried to lie, but his voice got drowned out by the shouts filling the cabin.

"That's my purse!" cried an incredulous voice from somewhere behind me. Her voice was joined by others and a stampede began with celebrities looking to reclaim their possessions.

Stopping them wasn't easy, but Mike's voice did the trick.

"STOP!" His roar had the volume and authority required to give the crowd pause. More quietly, he continued, "Please allow us to identify your items so we can ensure the correct possession goes to the right person. Also," he held up an index finger, "it is necessary that the lieutenant here," he indicated Deepa, "records photographic evidence and takes statements from you. I apologise, but it is going to take a few minutes to sort this out. Please bear with us."

It was Mike Atwell as I remembered him. I had no idea why he was here and why he wouldn't have knocked on my door the moment he came aboard. How long ago did he join the cruise for that matter? If it was weeks, I was going to be mightily upset that he stayed away. Not for long though; he wasn't a person I could stay mad at.

Grumbling, whining, and general complaining arose from the celebrities and others who just wanted their things back. They were 'their' things after all. It wasn't until Mrs Ross cleared her throat and requested an apology that they simmered down.

"I should be the first to apologise," I bowed my head and offered my hand. "I was too quick to assume the worst of you."

"Yes, you 'ing were."

Liberty leaned her head toward her boyfriend, whispering, "What does 'ing mean? Is that a word?"

The boyfriend shrugged.

Asking the crowd at the door to make space, I left Deepa on her radio calling for reinforcements, and led the Ross family outside. I caught Mike's eye as I left, making sure he would follow.

Escaping the press of people just as three members of the ship's security team came running past on their way to help, I expressed again my most heartfelt apology.

"I will speak to the captain," I added, "to ensure the cruise line suitably compensates you for this terrible misunderstanding."

Helen surprised me by waving a dismissive hand.

"That won't be necessary. We're just here to see our Betty get hitched. She's happy and that's all that matters. Have you sorted out the business with John yet? I heard people saying he is no longer thought to be the killer, is that right?"

"Yes. Mercifully, I was able to prove his innocence. I'm afraid I still need to catch the real killer."

"Do you know who it could be?"

"No," I lied. My team was in place and would be watching, but catching The Mouth in the act was a whole different thing. Was there a way to prompt him into acting?

A little itchy feeling crept across my skull; a devious plan forming. Catching myself pulling my so-called devious face again, I reset my expression to neutral.

"Are you sure there isn't anything I can do for you, Mrs Ross?"

She placed a friendly hand on my shoulder. "Just make sure nothing else disrupts the 'ing wedding, please. It would be nice if it could just 'ing go according to 'ing plan now."

I could not agree more.

With one more apology – I just couldn't help myself – I let the Ross family go and turned my attention to Mike Atwell. He met me with a cross-eyed grin, then whacked the side of his head to knock his eyes back to normal. It wasn't like him to play the clown. In fact, I'd only ever seen him do it when it was just the two of us.

Hooking my hand into his elbow, I said, "Come along, Detective Sergeant Atwell. You've got some explaining to do."

The Question He Needed to Ask

"Indeed I do," he agreed. "It's Mr Atwell now for a start."

"You quit?" I spun around to face him, causing us both to stop walking.

I found him to be grinning, his eyes fixed somewhere else; on a memory perhaps.

"I did. Did you, um ... did you read about a chap called Albert Smith and a crazy maniac member of the royal family called Earl Bacon?"

"The Gastrothief? Yes." I had read about it and watched the news with great gusto because I knew Albert Smith personally. I knew his late wife better – Petunia had always been in church on a Sunday whereas Albert would show his face perhaps once a month. They were a lovely couple though and I remembered their children being in school around the same time as me. My brain catching up with itself, I sensed why Mike had asked the question. With a gasp, I asked, "Were you involved?"

Mike's smile looked to be etched permanently onto his face. "Kind of. On the fringe perhaps."

I took that to mean he was directly in the midst of the adventure, for Mike was never one to talk about his triumphs.

"I met Albert at a wedding venue in Kent. There was a warrant out for his arrest at the time, but I chose to tread a different path. I guess I could tell he was not only innocent but that his outlandish claims about a hidden criminal mastermind were true. Instead of slapping the cuffs on, I let him go. It cost me my badge and almost my pension, but it was the right thing to do."

We were promenading around the ship, taking a leisurely stroll back to my suite where I would consider my next move in the apprehension of The Mouth. I had a devious plan, but would need help to pull it off.

When Mike ended his tale about the events in Wales, treating me to a first-hand account of Albert Smith's exploits, I had a serious question to ask him.

"What will you do now, Mike? Have you got something lined up?"

He steered me to the edge of the deck, releasing my hand to grab the railing with both of his. He was looking out to sea, a wistful set to his face. He stayed like that for a few seconds, making me think he was pondering something deep or building up to say something that was going to be hard to get out.

However, when he turned to face me, he appeared serenely relaxed and happy.

"If you cast your mind back several months, Patricia, you may remember offering me custody, if that's the right word, of your private investigations business."

Overjoyed at what he was asking, even though he hadn't asked it yet, I clapped my hands together and grabbed him for a hug.

"Yes, Mike! Yes, yes, yes! Please, I want you to take over the business. The office is just sitting there vacant." I was so pleased to hear he would be working for himself. Pushing out of the hug so I could see his face, I asked, "Wait, is that why you came here? Is that why you are on board?"

"Yes. I know I could have phoned, but this sort of thing ... well, I believe it requires discussion in person."

I got what he was trying to say, but had to argue, "I'm not sure what there is to discuss, Mike. The business is yours. I'll make some calls tomorrow to have the office keys delivered to your house and have the lease signed across."

"But what about your cut of the takings? It's your business."

"Ha! Don't be ridiculous, Mike. I'm not taking a penny. Whatever you make is yours. Change the business cards, rename the business ... or don't if you think having my name on the door will help attract clients. Entirely your call, but the whole thing is yours, every last bit of it."

Mike looked like he wanted to argue but he didn't. He put his hand out to meet mine and we shook on it.

Hooking his arm once more, I steered him back toward the doors to go inside. It was cool out and I was thirsty, hungry, and keen to take my shoes off.

"Come on. I have some friends I want you to meet."

Friends Together

"Oh," said Felicity, evidently surprised to see him. "Hello, Mike. What are you doing here?"

I blinked. "Wait. You two know each other?"

Mike stepped in close enough to air kiss Felicity and stepped back again.

"We've met." He did not elaborate.

"Hi, Mike," said Mindy, coming off a phone call and giving her aunt a thumbs up before using a pen to tick something off the clipboard resting in her lap.

We were back in my suite where Felicity and Mindy were having a better time of it than they expected. The calls to florist, harpists, exotic pet providers – for the swans apparently, ice sculptors, and many, many more were received with relief in most cases. The crew assigned to set up the wedding venue and the banquet hall for the event itself were easy enough to reengage so in just a couple of hours the whole thing had performed its third (or was it fourth) U-turn in twenty-four hours.

They were nearing the end and relieved that they might yet pull off the impossible and give the bride and groom the wedding of their dreams.

Mike already knew Jermaine and Barbie, but not Lady Mary except by name because her family were famous in the small corner of the world from which we hailed.

Dinnertime came around, a sumptuous feast of scallops and enormous prawns in linguini with a creamy, saffron sauce. Accompanied by garlic bread and washed down with a white wine that was like drinking velvet, I ate more than I should and had to surreptitiously unbutton the top snap on my trousers.

Jermaine, the evil git, then produced a tiramisu – one of my all-time favourite desserts and I had to have a slice. I mean, he'd gone to all that trouble. It would have been rude not to.

Conversation centred on the horror of the Ross family's ordeal and how cruelly they were targeted (and how bad I felt), but swung to focus on Mike and his reason for visiting. There was much congratulating and he got to regale the table with his tale about Albert Smith and the Gastrothief again.

All too soon the meal was done and I had to get back to the task of catching a killer.

"I can help," volunteered Mike. "I can get close to the suspect if that will help. No one knows me here. Everyone knows you."

I grinned. "Everyone knows Patricia Fisher. No one knows Gloria."

Barbie's eyes doubled in size. "You're not seriously planning to include mad granny, are you?"

I couldn't help the laugh that burst from my lips.

Mike leaned to his left to ask Lady Mary, "Who's Gloria?"

Lady Mary just shrugged and took a swig of gin.

It was the first I'd heard Barbie refer to Gloria as 'mad granny'. It fit though. Sam Chalk's grandmother came on board to help look after Sam Chalk. He doesn't need a lot of supervision, but she is there to make sure his laundry gets done and his uniform is presentable. That doesn't take up all that much of her time though and she can be a bit of a handful. Most recently, she took ownership of a mobility scooter and used it to run over some people I happened to be chasing.

Well, she wasn't going to be getting up to mischief on it tonight because I was going to borrow it.

Probably.

First, I needed to see how the team was doing and whether they were making any progress.

"None at all," replied Lieutenant Commander Martin Baker when I called him. "The Mouth spent the last three hours in his cabin with his girlfriend. The ex-wives have been returned to their cabins with their escorts for now. If he leaves, I will … hold on. His door just opened. Wait."

I had Martin on speakerphone so everyone could hear the call. My friends were crowded around to hear.

"Yes, he's leaving. He's with his girlfriend. Looks like they are going to dinner. I'll follow and let you know where they go. Do we send the ex-wives to the same venue so he can see them?"

"Yes. I'll handle it. You stay on the suspect and keep out of sight."

Ending the call, I looked at Barbie.

"Ready?"

"You're sure about this? It went terribly last time."

I shrugged. "Practice makes perfect."

Old Lady Vibes

Barbie was not wrong in her claim that the last time I chose to dress as an older lady, the execution could have been better. The problem was my false teeth which I kept spitting out when I tried to talk. The solution: don't use them. They were an unnecessary prop in my opinion, and I would look convincing enough with the hair, dress, and makeup.

A call to Gloria got her to come to me. Sam was involved in the undercover spy operation already and undoubtedly loving it. Another of Sam's unique skills was that no one ever suspected him. If they caught him looking their way, they would either look away or wave/smile. His goofy grin disarmed people.

Gloria rolled into my suite on her scooter with a trio of dresses over her knees.

"I brought these for you to try on."

A wig, some makeup, a dress borrowed from a woman in her eighties, and the scooter ... it would convince most people until they looked more closely.

"Your boobs are too high," said Barbie, coming at me with her hands out.

I swiped them away. "Speak for yourself." Barbie's chest literally defies gravity.

"No, I mean they need to hang lower. Even if Gloria were wearing a push-up bra she wouldn't fill that dress the way you are."

Gloria agreed. "She not lying. Like spaniels ears they are now," she cackled. "Didn't used to be."

"All right. Okay. I can do it myself though, thank you."

I turned around to rearrange myself only to find Mike behind me. He aimed his eyes at the ceiling with a chuckle.

Huffing, I went to my bedroom where I fiddled around and eventually discarded my bra completely. A stretchy, strapless top positioned six inches lower than it ought to be did the trick and I returned to the suite's main living area to have the assembled guests inspect my chest.

"Happy now?"

"Much better," said Barbie.

"Superior," agreed Jermaine.

"Nice knockers," chuckled Mike, ducking away when I tried to swat his arm.

Makeup provided a few liver spots to my hands and the disguise was complete. It wouldn't fool anyone for long, but it didn't have to. I was banking on The Mouth stopping in one or more of the bars this evening as he prowled with his camera for fresh celebrity gossip footage. There I would run over his foot with Gloria's scooter and while apologising say something about how I loved his YouTube channel and thought he was right about John Oswald being guilty.

He wouldn't spill the beans right there and then. Well, I suppose he could, but having planned the double murders so cleverly, I doubted I was going to catch him out so easily. The idea was to prompt or goad him into action by pointing out or asking which of the two wives The Mouth thought John might kill next.

To be honest, I didn't have a script in my head. I was going to make it up on the spot and hope for the best.

We waited until Martin confirmed The Mouth was on the move.

"Ready, mother?" asked Mike; he was playing the role of my son to act as interference if needed.

Beeping the horn on Gloria's scooter, I flipped it into forward and set off.

Old Lady Fetish

The Mouth went to the Blue Banana Bar on deck seventeen because that's where a glut of the celebrities on board had chosen to gather. Martin had tailed him there with Pippin and Schneider, the three of them swapping places and hanging back so their target would not feel he was being followed.

My team members stayed outside; their task only to know where he was.

Sending Imelda and Carol to have dinner just a few tables from The Mouth and his girlfriend failed to generate the response I hoped for. According to Martin, who watched from the bar, The Mouth never once looked their way.

Lots of people stopped by his table – some for autographs, others because they were celebrities and wanted to act as though they were friends. I found it all very odd. The Mouth habitually embarrassed film stars, musicians, and public figures such as politicians by getting into their business and finding out the little secrets they wouldn't want anyone else to know.

In researching him in preparation for this evening, I learned he had recently caused a stir when he exposed a man touted to be a viable candidate for the US presidency as a homosexual. He was no such thing and there should have been no shame in it. However stalking him for weeks, The Mouth built up enough evidence of clandestine meets and photographs where he and his supposed lover were standing just that little bit too close that his party had already dropped his candidacy and distanced themselves.

In other examples, The Mouth just picked out something about a person and attacked it: They looked awful in a dress, they'd clearly been having too many happy meals and had gained ten pounds, their new hairstyle made them look like a clown. It was endless and when they reacted, he got even more footage and airtime.

To me he was the most loathsome of creatures: one who makes profit from the misery of others.

Getting to the Blue Banana Bar took longer than expected because I kept ramming the scooter into things. They look easy to control, but there is a knack to it.

Martin was waiting for me around the corner.

"He's at the bar with half a dozen famous people. That rapper, Death Pillow is in there with his entourage and you just missed Tom Hanks and his wife. Pippin managed to get a seat next to The Mouth's girlfriend so you can take it. He will move when you arrive."

I sucked in a deep breath. Doing risky undercover stuff where I go in close to a person I know to be a murderer always sounds good in my head. However, when the time comes, I find myself wishing I'd chosen to take a bath instead.

My legs felt weak, and it made me glad to be sitting down.

Too late now, I pulled the throttle and crept forward.

Inside the bar the atmosphere was electric. A large black man, probably Death Pillow, I guessed, was rapping freestyle about something funny because the people around him were laughing riotously.

Just inside the door, a TV personality I recognised but could not name – one of those who hosts game shows and the like – was holding court with anecdotes about the passes women coming on his shows would make.

FOUR EX-WIVES AND A WEDDING

Dead ahead lay the bar where I saw the petite form of Lieutenant Anders Pippin. He wore a garish shirt that matched the bar's décor and held a large blue goldfish bowl of cocktail in his right hand. Pretending to sip at it from a straw, he was listening to The Mouth. The gossipmonger's lips seemed never to stop. He wasn't chatting with the people around him though, not exactly. He was talking to the camera.

As always he had a little GoPro style camera on a handle and was talking to it. His girlfriend held another, neither of them in the bar to drink.

Eyes forward, I whispered to Mike, "Mind out."

I'm not sure he heard me, but I cranked the throttle on Gloria's scooter and shot forward.

Yeah, I shot forward all right. Totally out of control.

I got just time enough to yell, "Look out!" before I barrelled into a chair. The chair toppled and in true Patricia style I rode Gloria's scooter up it like a demented, geriatric Evil Knievel. Canted at a forty-five-degree angle, I teetered for a moment, the people in the bar looking my way in rapt fascination. Until the scooter toppled, and I fell off.

A passing waitress wasn't looking the right way and had to duck out of my way with a shriek of terror. The tray she held stood no chance and the drinks even less so. They went airborne, a round of brandies I discovered when they cascaded all over my head.

Coming to rest, the wrong way up with my backside in the air and the dress over my head, I prayed for the floor to swallow me.

The inevitable stunned silence gave way to raucous laughter when The Mouth cackled, "Hey, look, everyone! It's a full moon."

That he was referring to my backside and the enormous pants I'd chosen to go under the dress was in no doubt. Any chance I had to pull off the clever little line about John Oswald was already gone. My best bet was to get up and run from the bar, but as luck would have it, I didn't even get to do that.

Hands hooked under my arms, sympathetic people coming to rescue me. They saw a senior citizen face down on the floor in a bar and unlike The Mouth they were concerned for my wellbeing.

That would have been all well and good, but one of them, a young woman had a cocktail in her hand, one of the ones they put a sparkler in.

The moment she was close enough for the sparks to land on the neat brandy now soaked into my wig, it ignited.

Like when a chef tips his pan to flambé a dish and you get that 'whumf' of flame.

People screamed, me especially.

Someone shouted, "Put her out! Quickly!" and another voice yelled, "Grab the fire extinguisher!"

The onlookers thought it was my real hair on fire and were most shocked when I ripped the wig off and proceeded to stomp on it.

Silence settled, the people in the bar, every last one of them staring at the old lady who was now someone else. I could feel the makeup Barbie used sliding off my face. One of my boobs had popped out of the stretchy top I used to pin them lower than they should sit so now I had one at normal height and the other halfway to my belly button.

If Pippin's eyes were anything to go by, I looked an absolute state. It was time to make a fast exit. Stuff the scooter, I would send someone back for it later. I needed to get out of here, but even that didn't go to plan.

The Mouth, a man who prided himself on knowing everyone who's face ever graced a TV screen, recognised me.

"Oh, my God, you're Patricia Fisher!" he barked. Swinging his camera to frame me, he started speaking to his audience. "Ladies and gossipmongers, I promise you exclusives. I promise you action you can't get anywhere else, well how's this for a scoop?" He shifted angles to get a better shot of my face. "World famous sleuth, Patricia Fisher, has an old lady fetish. She likes to pick up younger men in bars by pretending to be a geriatric old hag."

"That's not ..." I started. Conscious I was being livestreamed to millions of people and would be forever enshrined in internet glory, I shut my mouth and thought about how I could possibly turn this around.

"She also likes showing the world her undercarriage," The Mouth talked to his audience. "I'm sure you all remember the way she fell off the stage at the Maharaja of Zangrabar's coronation. She's just done it again in here, probably to lure some poor, unsuspecting young victim back to her bedroom."

To my great horror he grabbed Pippin's arm.

"How are you feeling right now, young fellow? Are you nervous? Or are you here on purpose? Are you Mrs Fisher's snack for the night." The Mouth made a horrible eating sound into his microphone.

Mortified though I was, my ire was rising, and I'd had enough. It might not be the smartest play in the book, but I was going to do it anyway.

"No, Reuben. He's not here for me to pick up. He's here to spy on you."

That shut him up.

"That's your real name, isn't it? Reuben Horowitz Junior. Youngest son of Reuben and Alice Horowitz."

The Mouth smirked. "So you know my real name. So does anyone who cares to look it up. Big deal." He sounded as confident as ever, but I couldn't help notice that he'd stopped filming.

"Why did you ask John Oswald if he killed his wife?"

"Wives," The Mouth corrected me. "Isn't that the case? Two of John Oswald's ex-wives have met their end on this cruise since they came aboard yesterday. Why did I ask John if he killed them? Because it's what I do? I stir the pot, lady. Anyway, I was right, he did kill them. As I heard it, you arrested him this morning."

I twitched, desperate to announce that I knew he was the killer. I could throw it down right now and see how he responded. I truly wanted to, but I managed to hold my tongue. Forcing a knowing smile onto my face, I found the opening I needed to goad him the way I had planned.

"Well, John has managed to throw sufficient doubt on his guilt. He's out, and while I continue to look for proof to tie him to the case, there is nothing I can do to keep him locked up right now. I'm sure you already heard the wedding is back on."

From The Mouth's face I could tell that was news to him. He'd spent the afternoon in his cabin with his girlfriend and then went to dinner. This last twenty minutes in the bar were probably the only ones where he could have been exposed to my revelation and it hadn't come up.

The Mouth looked confused. Was he about to question my sanity? Would he inadvertently tip his hand by questioning how it was that the bloody knife in John's cabin hadn't been enough to secure a conviction? Or the blood on his cuff which I assumed was rubbed onto his shirt by The Mouth in passing?

I wasn't so lucky. My revelation stunned him, but only for a brief moment. Two seconds was all he needed to recover.

"Well how about that for gross incompetence, ladies and gentlemen?" he addressed the bar. "A world famous sleuth and she can't even find the evidence to convict an old man guilty of killing his ex-wives."

I had to leave. Not because The Mouth still had the upper hand, but because if I stayed it would be me who tipped my hand, not the other way around.

Stalking from the bar with The Mouth caterwauling and cheering as he once again talked to his audience at home, I passed Mike.

He looked angry and embarrassed for me. Worried he might do something rash like punch The Mouth in the mouth to see if that would shut him up, I gripped Mike's arm and took him with me.

Pippin caught up to us outside pushing Gloria's scooter along by his side.

"That man is truly awful," he remarked.

It was probably intended to make me feel better, but I said nothing in return. I had nothing to say and there really was no reason to voice my thoughts. Far better to do what I said I would and catch him when he tried to frame John again.

The seed was sown. It might have cost me my dignity, but The Mouth now knew John found a way to wriggle out of custody. He was at large, but still under suspicion. If Reuben Horowitz Junior wanted to avenge his grandfather's death and send John Oswald to jail, he had one night in which to achieve it.

The Vital Clue

I awoke the next morning confused. My clock said 0700hrs and the alarm had just gone off. That couldn't be right. The team were supposed to call me when they caught The Mouth sneaking off to kill someone. I expected it would be either Imelda or Carol, but wasn't going to be surprised if the killer mixed it up and went after someone else. There were plenty of people connected to John on board the ship including some current and former business partners and rivals.

The ex-wives were left without a guard on their doors. Instead, there were security officers hidden inside their suites ready to pounce if The Mouth were to enter.

John had the same, just in case The Mouth decided the most expedient method of revenge was to kill the man he sought to frame.

Sitting up and yawning while I stretched my arms wide on either side of my body, I disturbed a warm lump by my left hip. It grumped and burrowed deeper. Using both hands I scooped it.

"Good morning, Anna," I kissed her head and popped her on the carpet, rummaging around under the covers to find her daughter. "And good morning, Georgie." She got a kiss too.

Throwing off the covers, I found a robe and went in search of coffee and answers.

The suite was devoid of life which was most unusual. Normally Jermaine would be up and about at the very least. Quite often it was Barbie too. She was a big fan of early morning workouts to start the day the right way.

I recalled her saying she was bunking with her boyfriend, Hideki, because he had the night off. It explained her absence.

"Good morning, madam," Jermaine stood up from behind the kitchen counter just as I got to it, scaring the life out of me. He was dressed in his official butler's outfit and had been out of sight to sweep something from the deck.

He had a dustpan and brush in his hands which he emptied into a small bin out of sight from where I leaned on the back of a barstool hoping my heart would continue beating.

"Were there no callers in the night?" I asked.

Jermaine shook his head. "No, madam. You were expecting to hear from Lieutenant Commander Baker?"

"Yes. Him or anyone else from the team. This is most disappointing." There were more than twenty of the ship's security team involved in the operation last night, most of them volunteers because, apparently, it's cool to work on Mrs Fisher's team.

"Can I offer you some coffee, madam?"

I nodded, said thank you, and settled onto the barstool.

The sound of a door opening pulled my head around to see Felicity exiting her room. She was dressed for a wedding with an elegant dress, sheer stockings and elegant heels. In her hair she wore a fascinator that sparkled and caught the light in the room.

"Good morning," she greeted me. "Big day today."

"The wedding isn't for hours," I questioned. "Why are you up so early?"

"Oh, I can never sleep before one of my weddings. There's always so much to do and as 'the' wedding planner, I like to make sure I am at hand to smooth all the creases that occur."

"Where's Mindy?"

"Probably fast asleep and snoring like a warthog. She has no such trouble with nerves."

Jermaine handed us both mugs of freshly brewed coffee and enquired about breakfast. Felicity said she couldn't possibly eat, she was far too nervous, and I felt an overwhelming need to check in on my team.

Fervently hoping they had The Mouth in custody and had caught him with a dagger in his hand as he crept through someone's room to extend his murder spree, I had a sickening feeling that would not be the case.

"He never left his room, Mrs Fisher," Martin gave me the bad news. "From the Blue Banana Bar The Mouth visited the Karaoke bar on deck sixteen where his presence with a camera was enough to stop all the celebrities lining up to sing. Even the professional singers wouldn't get on stage with him around. He visited five other bars after that and returned to his cabin at 0112hrs. He is still there now."

I heard Martin trying to kill a yawn.

"Have you been up all night?"

"Yes. Someone had to coordinate it all. I just wish there had been something to do."

So did I. Did I have it wrong? Was the death of his grandfather not the catalyst I assumed it to be, and the killer was still unidentified?

"Is there someone to take over from you?"

"There is. I'm about to hand over to Deepa. I've stood Molly down too. The bride's family are all around her already, no one is going to get to Miss Ross today. Molly had a full night's sleep so she can take over watching The Mouth's cabin with Deepa. Do I remove the guards from their posts inside the ex-wives' cabins?"

"Yes. I see no reason for them to remain there. Leave a man on the doors and …" My skull itched.

"Mrs Fisher?"

"Martin what were the names of the two men who were on the door of Fiona Sugarman's suite around the time she was murdered?" I held my breath, waiting for an answer.

"Um." I could almost hear Martin scrunching his fatigued brain to wring the information from it. "Err, it was Ensign Roach and Lieutenant Gallagher. Did you not speak to them already?"

"No, I never got the chance." I'd meant to, but more pressing things got in the way. I could remember telling Martin to stand them down. "How soon can you find them?" I asked the question while hustling back to my bedroom. Anna and Georgie were tailing me, wondering what had happened to their breakfast.

"Ah, give me a couple of minutes." Martin hung up and was probably on his radio by the time I closed my bedroom door.

"Mummy will feed you in a minute, ladies," I assured the dogs. They danced around thinking that might mean now and were disappointed when I sat at my dressing table and took stock. I needed makeup and an outfit if I was to leave the suite.

Grabbing a brush, I started on my hair.

Martin came back to me in under a minute.

"They were both volunteers for last night's operation. Sorry, I should have remembered that."

"It's okay. Sleep deprivation is a terrible thing for the memory."

"Well, they were in Carol Oswald's suite, so I told them to come straight to you. They should be there in a few minutes."

I swore inside my head and yanked open a drawer to find fresh underwear. I was mostly dressed by the time they arrived. Making them wait wasn't in my nature, but a lady of a certain age needs time to make herself look presentable.

Content with my hair, makeup, and choice of outfit, I sent the dogs to find Jermaine and asked him to feed them while I aimed myself at the men now rising from my chairs.

"Mrs Fisher," they said in unison.

"Thank you for coming. I'm sure you would like to get some breakfast and a little shut eye, but I need to know if anyone came or went from Mrs Sugarman's suite while you were guarding it."

They both shook their heads and Lieutenant Gallagher said, "We went through this thoroughly with Lieutenant Commander Baker, Mrs Fisher. No one came in or out at any point. We both stood our watch outside the door for the entire period. I was there from ten until eleven when Ensign Roach relieved me. He was there until Midnight when Lieutenant Singh took over. Sorry, Ms Fisher, I realise that's not helpful, but I don't know what to tell you."

Ensign Roach stayed quiet the whole time and when I flicked my eyes across to his, he looked away.

Facing him, I demanded, "Did you see The Mouth two nights ago? Did he come by Mrs Sugarman's suite and convince you to step away from the door?"

"What? No!"

His reply was instant, but it was missing something. It had the ring of truth, yet it was also hollow, like he was holding something back. I made a leap.

"Was she pretty?" I asked. I got a 'huh?' expression in return. "The woman who distracted you the night Mrs Sugarman was killed, was she pretty?"

"I don't ..."

FOUR EX-WIVES AND A WEDDING

I cut him off. "You don't know what I'm talking about? At the moment you are guilty of lying to your superiors. The dereliction of duty charge sits on top of that, but failing to come forward with the truth now will end your career before it gets started. I need to know who she was, Ensign Roach. If it wasn't a woman, tell me who it was." My voice was firm and unyielding. I was going to start yelling if I needed to.

Guilt clung to the young Ensign now. He'd covered up his failing with lies and probably believed he would get away with it.

Fortunately for me, Lieutenant Gallagher wasn't about to stick up for his fellow security officer. He could smell the guilt just as clearly as me.

Glaring at his subordinate, he demanded, "Well? Go on, man. The truth this time."

Flinching from the power of our combined gazes, he blurted, "I ... I don't know who she is? She was drunk though."

Gallagher tried to press Roach for more until my hand on his arm stopped him.

"Let him tell us what happened," I encouraged.

Roach, a big man though still barely more than a boy, was on the verge of tears and stuttered when he spoke.

"I ... I didn't know what to do. I mean, I couldn't undo what had happened. I didn't see anything ... I just ... I just ... I had to step away."

A frown creased my forehead. "Step away? What does that mean?"

Lieutenant Gallagher threw up his arms in exasperation. "What were you thinking, man? You never step away from the post! Never. If you get caught short, or see something that demands you react, what do you do?"

Roach's head was bowed, his eyes refusing to meet ours when he mumbled quietly, "I use my radio."

"Yes, you use your radio!" Gallagher agreed.

"Roach." I said his name softly, needing him to look at me and repeated it like a reassurance it was all going to be okay. When he looked up, I said, "Why did you step away? What happened?"

His lips twitched, one corner turning down as he wrestled with what to say.

"Damn it, man!" I snapped. "Tell me now or I will have Lieutenant Gallagher throw you in the brig!"

"A drunk girl threw up on me!" his words came out as one, bursting from his mouth in a torrent.

Gallagher's nose wrinkled in disgust, and he said, "You were in pristine dress whites when I relieved you." His brow furrowed, the truth dawning on him. "You didn't step away! You went back to your bunk to get changed!"

"I stank!" wailed Roach. "It was all down my tunic and on my trousers and it was making me wretch. It stank like tequila and coconut."

I had some sympathy for the man, but nothing could negate the fact that he abandoned his post. Covered in vomit, one use of his radio would have supplied a replacement in moments. Drunk passengers were an occupational hazard.

I pushed all that to one side. My skull itched like mad and I knew what I had just heard was the killer creating a diversion to get into Fiona Sugarman's cabin. I already had a good idea who the 'drunk' woman was. Now I needed to hear it from Roach.

"The woman, Roach, what did she look like?"

Thirty seconds later, I was running, my radio in my hand as I yelled instructions into it.

"I've got him! Meet me at The Mouth's cabin as fast as you can get there!"

My message addressed my private team of security officers, the ones assigned to work with me to solve whatever crimes occurred on board. Deepa, Schneider, Molly, Sam, and Anders were all converging on the same spot I now raced toward. Martin was already there.

Slightly out of breath when she spoke, Deepa asked, "What was it? What changed?"

Equally out of breath ... oh, who am I kidding? I could barely find the air to utter the words, but managed to gasp, "The Mouth got his girlfriend to throw up over Ensign Roach when he was guarding Mrs Sugarman's door. Roach went to get changed, the poor fool. He identified her though. I'm sure it's her." I took a break to get some air in my lungs. "I don't know her name, but I think we can assume she was there deliberately to help The Mouth frame John."

Martin's voice came on the line the moment I released my send button.

"There's a fight going on inside. It's getting heated."

"Wait for the rest of us!" shouted Deepa. "I'm five minutes away!"

His voice tinged with concern, Martin said, "Something just smashed against the wall inside. I'm going in."

"Is anyone closer?" I asked, hearing the anxiety I felt in my words.

A round of 'No's' confirmed my fears. The ship is a vast place, like a city stacked one deck atop the other twenty times. Even with the elevators it could take an age to get from one of the lower decks or the wrong end of the ship to any particular point.

Deepa wouldn't get to Martin for five minutes and I expected that to prove to be a hopeful guess. It meant I was the closest. Still two minutes away myself, I begged Martin to wait.

"I can't," he replied, iron will in his voice as he prepared for what lay beyond the door to The Mouth's cabin. "He may be trying to hurt her. I'll not cower outside to discover I could have prevented injury or worse."

"But you're not armed!" Deepa shouted. Unwilling to be stopped, Martin announced he was entering the cabin and was gone from the airwaves, his radio away to leave his hands free.

Like everyone else, I waited for his voice to come back on the line, so we knew he was okay and had the situation under control. I ran on, my lungs screaming for me to stop. My legs began to tire, the muscles starting to ache as the flow of oxygen-rich blood dwindled. I couldn't get enough air into my body, but I didn't want to slow down.

Running for a few minutes might not sound like much, but let me assure you trying to go as fast as you can soon wears a person out. Additionally, being on the ship adds obstacles in the form of passengers, so it becomes more like a parkour course than a straight run. Ducking around families, leaping plants, zipping through gaps and bouncing off bulkheads when my route demanded a ninety degree turn down a new passageway all took more from me than I had to give.

Still nothing from Martin and I had no air left in my lungs to use my radio. Not that I needed to because Deepa yelled for him to answer constantly.

With mounting fear, I careened into the final turn. The door to The Mouth's suite was ahead of me on the left. I reached it ten seconds later to be greeted by a sight I never want to see again.

Martin was on the carpet two yards inside the door. His hands were pressed over a wound on his abdomen where bright red blood oozed between his fingers. He'd been stabbed!

In his own clothes for the stakeout operation last night, he didn't have his sidearm with which he could have defended himself and The Mouth had come at him with a knife.

Heaving air into my body, I fell to my knees at his side. I had my radio to my mouth though I was barely able to speak.

Martin's eyes were open and etched with pain. Between his lips, his teeth were clenched tight shut.

"Bedroom," he wheezed, his teeth never parting.

Gasping in a breath, I held the radio to my mouth and called for help. I needed urgent medical assistance for a member of crew. Cringing, because I knew Deepa would hear it, I told the paramedics the victim had been stabbed.

Then, with a grunt of effort to get myself moving, I ran to the bedroom to find The Mouth's girlfriend. Was that why Martin sent me here? Was she in an even worse state than him? Would there be anything I could do to save her?

The Horrifying Truth

Horrified for what I might find, I would have held my breath had such a thing been possible. As it was, I could barely hear myself think over my laboured gasps of air. Nevertheless, it was no exaggeration to say the sight of The Mouth lying in a pool of his own blood took my breath away.

Fluttering hands rose to my mouth, my legs weak until his eyes moved to look at me.

He was alive!

Propped against a wall, his head lolling to one side, the front of his shirt was stained bright red with fresh blood that ran down to his waist.

His wound was to his chest, and anyone could see he was losing the fight to stay conscious. Frozen to the deck just inside the doorway, his eye movement jolted me into action.

His pale face turned to look up at me.

"Sarah. It was Sarah," he wheezed. "She killed John's ex-wives."

I fell to my knees by his side and gripped his left hand. "Shhh, don't talk. Save your energy. Help is coming."

"Smile," he said, "You're live streaming to the world."

FOUR EX-WIVES AND A WEDDING

I turned to gawp at his right hand which, as always, held the GoPro camera.

"This might be my last show, but it will be the one that breaks the internet," he managed with a smile. Turning the camera so it was aimed at his face he wheezed, "Well folks, things caught up with me. I want you all to know, Patricia Fisher is a true lady. Despite all the terrible things I said to her, she's here trying to save me."

I pushed his right arm down to get the camera away. There was worryingly little resistance from the big man.

"Please stop talking," I begged. "Help will be here soon. Just stay with me."

"Too late," his voice came as a whisper. "Can't help me now. Need you to know, she did it for me."

I grabbed the radio again, all but cursing into it in my demand that help arrive sooner. A squeeze, almost too weak to feel, came from The Mouth's hand on mine.

"She did it for me, but I..." He stopped speaking to try to draw a breath. There was no colour left in his cheeks now and the light seemed to be fading from his eyes, "but I didn't want this. I told her about my grandfather. About how John caused his death and ruined my family." He shuddered like a person suffering from terrible, penetrating cold and went still. His eyes glazed and for a moment I thought he was gone. "She did it as a gift," his words came out on a breath, so faint I could barely hear them above the banging of blood in my head. "She stabbed me because I wasn't pleased." A smile cracked across his lips though it failed to reach his eyes. "Can you believe that?"

"Where is she Reuben?" I used his real name, trying to convince him to stay with me. "Where did she go?"

The sound of feet pounding down the passageway outside confirmed help was finally coming, the sound of paramedics arriving at speed in the suite's main room like music to my ears.

Martin croaked, "In the bedroom. Mrs Fisher is in the bedroom," which sent one of them to me.

"Let me get to him," demanded the paramedic, a young American woman of Chinese descent called Maisy as she barrelled into the room.

Moving, but having to shuffle to get my legs back under my body to get up, I squeezed the hand of Reuben Horowitz Junior one more time.

"Where did she go, Reuben? Tell me."

His eyes were no longer looking at anything and when I looked at his chest I could see no rise and fall. Tears brimmed in my eyes, the horror of it all overwhelming me, but I almost left my skin when he spoke again.

"John," he whispered. "She's going after John."

The words hammered into me like bullets. That I had managed to read the whole thing wrong tore at my soul. It wasn't the Mouth behind it all, much as I wanted it to be, it was his girlfriend and she had claimed another victim through my lack of vision. Maybe two; I thought of Martin.

Now I don't recall what I said to Maisy the paramedic or to Martin as I sprinted from the cabin. In fact, I don't really remember leaving The Mouth's suite, but time passed, and I was running again, belting headlong back through the passageways to get to John.

With radio in hand, I diverted everyone to the Platinum Suite. Not just my team, but everyone. Security officers, whether on duty or off, the rest of the crew, Jermaine and Barbie, and my fairy godmother if she felt like answering the call.

They would converge there and knew to expect a madwoman armed with a knife. The only question in my head was whether anyone could get there soon enough to save the eighty-two-year-old groom. I hadn't really paid any attention to The Mouth's girlfriend; she was just an attractive woman with jet black hair and a camera in her hand. I knew this though: she was lean and athletic. Her arms were all toned muscle and she was going to have no trouble overpowering John Oswald.

Was he alone? Was Tim with him? John was getting married today, so surely he would have a few of his closest friends by his side. But what did that mean? Would Sarah – I had no idea what her last name was – just stab and slash her way through them to get to her intended victim?

The worrying thought made me push harder just when I so desperately wanted to slow down.

As luck would have it, John's suite was significantly closer to The Mouth's than mine, so just more than a minute after setting off, I arrived breathless at his door. The short time required to cover the distance meant two things: Sarah had been able to cover it just as quickly and might have arrived here five minutes ago. Were that the case she could already be gone. Secondly, since I radioed for help as I ran, it had been only seconds since people started reacting and I was here first.

Common sense and the trifling fact that I was armed only with a cutting wit and a handbag, dictated I ought to wait. An armed security officer would be along any second now.

I couldn't hear anyone though.

Much like Martin, I wasn't prepared to stand outside in fear while inside people were being murdered. I couldn't hear anything – no sounds of fighting or shouting, and fearing the worst, I swiped my universal doorcard and shouldered open the door.

Dead End

My entrance interrupted a standoff and broke the spell. Expecting that John might have his eldest son, Tim, with him and perhaps one or two old friends, I was surprised to see Felicity and Mindy. Tim was there too and sporting a cut to his right arm and Bartholomew the butler was lying unconscious on the carpet just inside the door.

Blood dripped from Tim's right arm to the thick carpet where it pooled and would stain. Nevertheless, he held his ground, standing next to Mindy where the two of them blocked Sarah's route to the one she wanted to kill.

Felicity held tight to John, keeping him away from Sarah who held a nine-inch kitchen knife stained with red. She looked poised to leap when I pushed through the door, and did just that at the moment Mindy looked my way.

I screamed in horror, terrified I was about to witness another murder, but I'd forgotten Felicity's niece was a skilled martial artist.

Mindy feigned a strike only to duck and come up clutching Sarah's wrist. For a heartbeat, I thought it was all over. Mindy would disarm the woman and knock her senseless, if necessary, but that's not what happened at all.

Just as Mindy tried to break Sarah's grip on the weapon, the madwoman delivered a hammer blow to Mindy's ribs using her other hand.

Clearly Mindy didn't see it coming either for she cried out and lost her grip, only narrowly escaping the tip of the blade when Sarah swung it at her face.

Mindy growled at her pain as if that would scare it away, and changed her stance.

"No way you are getting to him, lady," the teenage ninja promised.

Sarah screeched in maddened rage, "I'll kill you all!" and lunged forward.

Mindy, dressed for the wedding in a tight dress that allowed only small leg movements, hitched the lower half to her waist in a single movement to show the world her knickers as she sidestepped, falling and spinning to sweep at the woman's feet with a scything leg. Sarah, clearly a skilled fighter in her own right, anticipated the move and leapt out of the way. When she landed, the distance she gained gave her the scant seconds she needed to finish the job.

Mindy flipped herself off the deck to land on her feet, but by then Sarah was running at John with the knife hand up and ready to strike. The only thing between her and the groom was Felicity and the already injured Tim.

They both moved to intercept, but I could tell they wouldn't be able to stop her.

The sound of a shot from behind me sucked the air from my body, the explosion of sound energy hitting me like a bat.

Sarah twitched, the arm held high in the air seemingly losing its momentum as though she had forgotten what she was supposed to be doing and needed a moment to gather her thoughts. She hung like that for a second, not moving.

Felicity, Tim, and John were still cowering away from the raised blade, looking for a way to escape it when Sarah's knees buckled and she fell.

Crumpling into a heap, the knife rolled out of her lifeless hand just before Mindy reached her. Forced to slow for she was about to pile through the madwoman's back, Mindy crouched to flick the blade out of reach. Then she felt at the woman's neck, staring down at Sarah's inert form when she shook her head.

I turned to find Deepa in the doorway. She held her sidearm in both hands; a classic pose with both arms forming a vee in front of her body. A wisp of smoke rose from the barrel.

She wasn't breathing, but as I realised that, she sucked in a deep, gasping breath. Holding it so she could take the shot, despite running to get to John's suite, she needed air in her lungs now and sagging into the door frame, she sobbed and looked like she might collapse.

"She killed Martin!" she cried between gasps.

More running feet heralded a platoon of security officers, Sam, Anders, and Molly among them.

I took Deepa to one side, my arms around her shoulders to get her to a chair. I felt weak myself, but the need to rest had been replaced by the knowledge that I was in charge and Deepa needed me.

Everyone heard Deepa's announcement and the mood in the suite was sombre, filled with pain, and punctuated by Deepa's sobs. Molly and Sam were crying too and I should have been but the tears failed to come.

It was minutes later when Alistair arrived that we discovered the truth.

Deepa heard Maisy the paramedic on the radio when she said her patient was gone and assumed she was talking about Martin. She didn't know The Mouth had been stabbed too and with all the horror, running, different locations, and Deepa's uncontrollable tears, I hadn't thought to mention it.

I was the only one in the cabin who had been to both suites.

Deepa lifted her head. There was a thread of hope she didn't dare grab hovering tantalisingly in the air.

Seconds later, we had Martin on the radio, telling his wife he was alive. Dr Hideki Nakamura was with him, and he was going to be fine. Sarah's blade caught an artery in his gut, and he needed surgery right now. He would live though; there appeared to be no question about that.

Deepa departed at a run to get to her husband. I sent Molly and Anders to stay with her and turned my attention back to Felicity, Mindy, Tim, and the groom.

The suite had filled with all the people I called. Jermaine assisted Bartholomew – now conscious and refusing medical attention - to prepare refreshments. Honestly, it was a crazed scene of carnage one moment and almost a relaxed cocktail party the next. Not that people were drinking. Well, not many were.

John certainly was, but assured me he was all right and joked that it was no worse than an average day on Wall Street. Tim's wound, while nasty, wasn't life threatening. He would recover, but more importantly, he was fine to act as best man this afternoon.

Dr Davis was in the suite to confirm Sarah was dead and there were paramedics, a different pair to those I met in The Mouth's suite to tend to Tim's injury.

Felicity had a glass of John's bourbon in her hand. Truthfully, it made me a little jealous – I wouldn't mind a hefty shot of something to calm my nerves – and Mindy was over by the window staring out to sea.

"Is she all right?" I asked.

Felicity belted the rest of the glass and shuddered. "She will be. She didn't like that she wasn't able to stop the crazy woman with the knife. I think she feels like she failed."

"But that's crazy."

Felicity shrugged. "I know. Actually, I think she might be seething slightly about having to leave her weapons behind. She usually has a set of nunchucks or a pair of sais hidden about her clothing."

"Doesn't sound comfortable," I found myself remarking.

"Reassuring though if one knows how to use them."

Our thoughts were interrupted by Barbie, who came to see if we needed her for anything. There was a wedding in just a couple of hours and with the wedding planner here drinking her frayed nerves away, I guessed nothing much was getting done.

"Oh, no, it's all right on track, actually," Felicity reassured me. "A few final bits to check, but the band arrived by helicopter first thing this morning. Stu Dapples says he is all set up for the party after the wedding breakfast, and provided everyone fits into their dresses and tuxedos, the only thing I have to worry about is the celebrities fighting with each other."

"You think they will?" asked Barbie, sounding curious.

Felicity looked about for somewhere to put her glass and said, "They always do. Celebrities are terrible for it. I think it's all to do with their egos. Anyway, I probably ought to be getting on with something. You don't need us?"

She called to Mindy while I said, "I'll get statements from you tonight, or tomorrow before you leave. What time is your flight?"

"Ten past ten tomorrow night. It will give Mindy some time to do the tourist thing. She wants to go up the Empire State Building and ride the Metro to Staten Island. Oh, and eat somewhere called Katz's Deli. Apparently, they are famous for their sandwiches," she added with a 'who knows' shrug.

Mindy joined her looking none the worse for her fight with a knife-wielding madwoman and the two left John's suite bound for whatever task Felicity had in mind.

A hand on my shoulder turned out to be Alistair.

"Are you all right, Patricia?" he asked, turning me around and wrapping his arms around me. "You spend your time worrying about everyone else. Let me take care of you."

I laid my head against his chest, comforted by the heartbeat I found there.

"I'm fine," I lied, knowing I was still shaken. The Mouth had revealed his connection to John Oswald and the truth of his past to his girlfriend at some point. With them both dead I was never going to get a full picture, but surmised that he spoke about the aging billionaire with venom and blamed him for his family's lack of fortune. I could understand how that might go, and wondered how accurate a picture Reuben Horowitz Junior might have possessed. Watered down by the passing of generations, did he believe

John Oswald set out to ruin his grandfather? Had he but spoken to John on the subject, he would have heard the pain and regret in the elder man's voice.

Too late now and I questioned what The Mouth's legacy would be. How would the world remember him? I thought him to be vile, but the void he left would be filled by another, possibly worse, gossip monger.

His girlfriend, Sarah Hardcastle – I knew her full name now – either misinterpreted Reuben's desires when it came to John Oswald, or simply wanted a reason to kill. She died from a single bullet that destroyed her heart as it passed through her chest. According to Dr Davis she was likely dead before she hit the deck.

I let Alistair walk me back to my suite where he poured me a gin and sat with me for a while. Anna and Georgie were on my lap, snuggled in and sleeping within minutes.

To further distract me, for he knows me well enough to spot when I am wallowing in self-recrimination, he asked about my outfit for the wedding. It wasn't the first time he'd asked, and I was keeping it a secret.

To counter, a wry smile creeping across my face, I asked, "What are you wearing?"

He laughed. "The same thing I always wear," and wafted a hand at his dress uniform. "Only, not this one. I have a fresh one for the ceremony."

His radio chose that moment to squawk, a message for him that a helicopter was approaching the ship and requesting clearance to land. He frowned when he asked, "Is it scheduled?"

The reply came back, "No, sir." I could tell Alistair was about to question why they were bothering him – you can't just come and land on a cruise ship – when the man added, "It's been chartered by the Maharaja of Zangrabar, sir."

Aftermath

I didn't run – I was done with running for one day – but I will admit that my footsteps were faster than they might otherwise have been as I made my way up to the helipad. Alistair and I ran into Jermaine and Barbie just outside the suite, so they were with me too.

We waited for the sleek helicopter to land, but from behind a glass panel which is a lot easier on the hair, I can tell you. Watching for the door to open, I wasn't surprised to find a lone traveller exiting the bird. It wasn't the Maharaja, of course, it was an envoy and as I suspected he would be, he was here to see me.

I'm not a big one for following the news or for keeping up on current affairs around the world, but I do know what is happening at home and have one eye vaguely trained on Zangrabar since I feel a certain tie to that small, but rich nation. Despite that, I had no idea what message the man might be here to deliver.

Alistair greeted the man – an assistant to the Zangrabar Ambassador in New York – and led him away from the helicopter. We didn't go far though for the man was simply delivering a letter.

Actually, I guess it would be more accurate to call it a wedding invitation. The Maharaja, still in his teens, was getting married. It was in one month's time at the palace in Zangrabar, and I was to be a guest of honour along with Alistair and as many of my friends as I wished to include.

I felt a little giddy.

Letter duly delivered, the envoy bade us all a good day, returned to his helicopter, and was airborne moments later.

"We are going, right, Patty?" Barbie wanted to know. "I might need a loan to buy a dress worthy of such an event."

"Who said I was including you in my group of friends?" I shot back, trying to keep a straight face and failing.

Barbie narrowed her eyes at me until I laughed.

I looked down at the letter one more time, folded it back into its envelope and said, "Come on. We need to get ready for a wedding."

Alistair kissed me before he went in the opposite direction and I had to run (yes, more running) to catch Jermaine and Barbie.

It will come as no surprise when I tell you the wedding was a lavish affair. Alistair looked incredible in his pristine dress whites and performed the ceremony to join Betty and John as the Aurelia cruised by the Statue of Liberty. The sun shone as if Felicity had arranged it, and everything happened like clockwork.

The celebrities behaved themselves; I didn't hear a single raised voice at any point though I did choose to leave before the party after the sit-down banquet got started. I left the loud music and revelling to the younger people, insisting Jermaine stay with Barbie. They would enjoy the celebrity spotting if nothing else.

I'd managed to snag Tom Hank's autograph; that was enough for me.

The Aurelia sailed into New York with the sun setting, and while the party took place on board, the majority of the ship's passengers left to explore. We were to be in the famous city for two days – plenty of time to visit the sights and hear the sounds.

In the morning, Alistair would take me on a guided tour. I wasn't all that bothered about where we went, I was just happy to spend time with him.

Back in my suite, I sipped at my gin and tonic and chatted with Mike, Lady Mary, and Felicity. Felicity's duties were done, the wedding a complete success that was bound to bring in more business. Mindy wasn't with us and was last seen chatting with a minor, but rising, film star who boasted credits from the Marvel movies.

I hadn't figured things out fast enough to stop Reuben Horowitz Junior, AKA The Mouth, from meeting his end and I knew that would weigh heavily on my conscience. However, had I known what New York had in store for me, it might have been thoughts of survival that dominated my mind.

The End

Authors Note

Hello, Dear Reader,

It is the end of yet another book. Not counting my co-written stuff, I believe this is number seventy-nine. It is Patricia's twenty seventh outing and though I occasionally fear I am making the series too long, the demands that I keep going are almost daily.

I will say that Patricia and her characters are easy to write. Partly because they are so familiar now, but also because they are so much fun. For now, at least, there is no end in sight, and I have a bunch more stories already planned.

In this book I use a dentist drill to make holes in wine glasses. I drew on my own experience for this. The armed services like to get people together for drinks and dinner. A little conversation and a few toasts to the royal family et cetera for any excuse you fancy. Someone is leaving, someone got promoted, it's the anniversary of the Corp's formation ...

Anyway, the toasts in the army were always with port and I saw more than one port glass leaking red liquid onto the pristine white tablecloths where the garrison dentist had been engaged to make a few holes.

It happened to me once though the junior officers responsible decided doing it again was not in their best interests.

I also mention Katz's Deli which is a New York landmark and the place where Meg Ryan faked her orgasm in front of a crowd in the film *When Harry Met Sally*. I have only been to New York once and only bothered to visit one place: Katz's Deli. You may condemn me for that, but I was there by myself, I'm not a person who has any interest in seeing things in person that I have seen on TV a million times and, to be fair, I was writing a book the rest of the time. It was 2018 though I forget now which story it was.

What I can say is that the trip to the deli was worth it and I yearn to return.

Take care.

Steve Higgs

What's next for Patricia?

A Reason to Kill

When they found the body of a stowaway in the bowels of the ship, no one could have predicted the storm of trouble heading their way.

Three-hundred-year-old coins found with the dead man's meagre belongings point to a treasure thought lost to the ocean long ago. However, when the arrival of a murderous mystery figure forced Patricia and her friends to figure things out for themselves, they questioned if the trail they now follow might just lead to one of the greatest treasure finds ever recorded.

Some might call that exciting, but for the gang on board the Aurelia, they have another word: deadly. They are playing someone else's game and not only are the rules unclear, they are constantly one step behind.

In the Canaries, they were being spied on. In Rio they found only bodies instead of answers – the mystery man left no one alive to reveal his secrets. Arriving in New York, things are about to get a whole lot worse. But sometimes the only way to avoid trouble is to hit it head on.

Other Series by Steve Higgs

Albert Smith's Culinary Capers

Baking. It can get a guy killed.

When a retired detective superintendent chooses to take a culinary tour of the British Isles, he hopes to find tasty treats and delicious bakes ...

... what he finds is a clue to a crime in the ingredients for his pork pie.

His dog, Rex Harrison, an ex-police dog fired for having a bad attitude, cannot understand why the humans are struggling to solve the mystery. He can already smell the answer – it's right before their noses.

He'll pitch in to help his human and the shop owner's teenage daughter as the trio set out to save the shop from closure. Is the rival pork pie shop across the street to blame? Or is there something far more sinister going on?

One thing is for sure, what started out as a bit of fun, is getting deadlier by the hour, and they'd better work out what the dog knows soon, or it could be curtains for them all.

Felicity Philips Investigates

Marriage? It can be absolute murder.

Wedding planner for the rich and famous, Felicity Philips is aiming to land the biggest gig of her life – the next royal wedding. But there are a few obstacles in her way ...

... not least of which is a dead body the police believe she is responsible for murdering.

Out of custody, but under suspicion, her rivals are lining up to ruin her name. With so much on the line, she needs to prove it wasn't her and fast. But that means finding out who the real killer is ...

... without said killer finding out what she is up to.

With Buster the bulldog as her protector and Amber the ragdoll cat providing sartorial wit – mostly aimed at the dog - Felicity is turning sleuth.

What does a wedding planner know about solving a crime? Nothing. Absolutely nothing.

Pets Investigate

Sticking their noses where they are most definitely not wanted.

Despairing of their humans, these pets take it upon themselves to solve the cases they see as only cats and dogs can.

Whether they sniff out the clues or fool the criminals into thinking they are harmless pets to be ignored, Rex, Amber, Buster, and more enjoy escapades a-plenty in this fun collection of short stories.

Grab your copy and be ready for the fur to fly!

Free Books and More

Want to see what else I have written?

Go to my website - https://stevehiggsbooks.com/

Or sign up to my newsletter where you will get sneak peaks, exclusive giveaways, behind the scenes content, and more. Plus, you'll be notified of Fan Pricing events when they occur and get exclusive offers from other authors because all UF writers are automatically friends.

Copy the link it carefully into your web browser.

https://stevehiggsbooks.com/newsletter/

Prefer social media? Join my thriving Facebook community.

Want to join the inner circle where you can keep up to date with everything? This is a free group on Facebook where you can hang out with likeminded individuals and enjoy discussing my books. There is cake too (but only if you bring it).

FOUR EX-WIVES AND A WEDDING

https://www.facebook.com/groups/1151907108277718

About the Author

At school, the author was mostly disinterested in every subject except creative writing, for which, at age ten, he won his first award. However, calling it his first award suggests that there have been more, which there have not. Accolades may come but, in the meantime, he is having a ball writing mystery stories and crime thrillers and claims to have more than a hundred books forming an unruly queue in his head as they clamour to get out. He lives in the south-east corner of England with a duo of lazy sausage dogs. Surrounded by rolling hills, brooding castles, and vineyards, he doubts he will ever leave, the beer is just too good.

If you are a social media fan, you should copy the link below into your browser to join my very active Facebook group. You'll find a host of friends waiting there, some of whom have been with me from the very start.

My Facebook group get first notification when I publish anything new, plus cover reveals and free short stories, but more than that, they all interact with each other, sharing inside jokes, and answering question.

facebook.com/stevehiggsauthor

You can also keep updated with my books via my website:

g https://stevehiggsbooks.com/

Printed in Great Britain
by Amazon